Last Train
to Limbo

Last Train
to Limbo

PↃP

A PLAYBOY PRESS BOOK

Contents

Preface

Limbo, from the Latin word meaning fringe or edge, is that part of supernatural geography that lies on the borders of hell. Dante thought of it as a kind of no man's land where dwell eternally the praiseless and the blameless dead. In the *Orlando Furioso* of Ariosto, there is another limbo, the Limbus of the Moon, where all manner of things are treasured up —things like misspent time, vain efforts, vows never kept, desires that lead to nothing, the vanity of titles, flattery, and the empty promises of those men the world calls great.

In modern usage, *limbo* often implies a suspension of natural order, a frozen state, a dimension outside of time and space as we understand them. It is in this sense the word is used in the title of this book's opening story, the haunting *Last Train to Limbo*.

Limbos of various kinds are explored in the other stories you will find in the following pages. Some are awesome and terrifying; others are delightfully humorous. Some take place in the limbo of outer space; others in the even stranger limbo of inner space—that is to say, the human mind.

All of the stories originally appeared in PLAYBOY magazine. The authors include such famous masters of science fiction as Ray Bradbury, Arthur C. Clarke, Robert Bloch, Fredric Brown, Richard Matheson, as well as new talents such as Asa Baber and Thomas Baum, recently arrived on the literary horizon. Charles Beaumont, William F. Nolan, Italo Calvino, H. C. Neal, T. K. Brown III, Larry Niven, Theodore L. Thomas are also among the roster of fine writers whose contributions make this book one of the most luminous treasuries of science fiction to be found—in limbo or out of it.

—the editors of PLAYBOY

Last Train to Limbo

asa baber

There was the smell of urine, the smell of violets,
the wind of the dairy farms floating toward the city.
Along about, perhaps just before, certainly after
Newark, across the marsh, came the green stink of
sewage gases and gas gases and sulphur from our
great industries. Seated alone, riding backward, secretly fingering a proximate erection and smudging
his tan permanent-press pants with *The New York
Times* newsprint off his tan fingers, his golfer's fingers, his once baseball-batting, cub-scouting, now
account-counting fingers, Avery read and felt grief.

Oops. Grief? *De profundis?*

Well, not Wailing Wall grief. He didn't like him
that much. Now, today, of course, you couldn't say
that. Not for a while, not until it was back to
business for everyone. But life goes on, he sighed;
tempus fidgets.

Tempus fidgets?

It do, it do, at 42. Perhaps before (although
Avery could not directly testify to that, having lost
no one at all except a Princeton roommate killed in
a glider crash off the California coast—and he was
South American).

Violence, violence, where would it end? Why can't

people get along? Avery got along. Really. Oh, he had a temper—manly, vigorous, quick to rise and quick to forgive—and once he had hit his wife, and more than once he had wanted to. His son, a three-year-old thumb-sucker, lived in friendly terror of his spankings. His dog, a three-year-old boxer, appreciated any time that Avery found to spend with him. Avery was not violent. Pressured, yes, but violent?

Never. That much he knew. He lived and let live. He tried to do his job, and it wasn't easy. You try it sometime, counseling the greedy, the clever, the smelly. Sitting next to Stein, who ate onion sandwiches and yoghurt for lunch, ate at his desk so as not to miss an inch of ticker, not a symbol in lights, but Stein didn't gulp it up.

T.G.I.F. That's what Avery said. T.G.I.F. End of the week. There was just so much a man could take, and this one had been a lulu (a "woo-woo," according to his son; it was one of their jokes). His wife, for example, waking him up early, before dawn, not once but *twice,* two mornings running. First, "He's shot"; then, "He's dead." His wife, the plump romantic, who took care to cry below the noise level of the air conditioner so that Avery could get back to sleep.

So the previous two mornings had been rough. She didn't help by standing in the kitchen doorway and watching the television, all the while pretending to create his breakfast out of fresh-frozen, boxed, dehydrated and price-reduced materials. Avery threw his shoe across the living room and yelled at her and set the boy to crying (a fake cry, Avery suspected, the cry of the actor or the pansy, able to produce tears at any time, at any goddamn moment). What did it profit a man? To work hard, to protect his family, and all he receives is tears, burnt bacon and a black scar on the newly painted beige wall. Oh, the mornings. Tomorrow of his mornings would be worse. He would be home all day.

"Kenny shot?"

"What, tiger?"

"Kenny shot?"

"Naaaw." He turns to his wife. "You've had him in front of the tube all day?" She nods and almost cries. "Jesus Christ." And it is the end of the day, when all souls need a drink, but Avery rises with an effort of the will that he sees as gallant, puts on his happy face and picks the boy up for a cuddle. Reverses his field, too. "Yes, he's shot." A big hug and rib tickles. The dog sheds on his pants leg, waiting for their sometime evening fight, in which Avery slaps him on his slobbery jowls and laughs and laughs.

"Kenny shot. Will I get shot?"

"Naaaw."

The boy becomes cute, all-knowing (well, then, he's forgotten it, hasn't he?). "Someday I might get shot. Yes, sir." Said with a righteousness that is endearing. Avery pulls his wife to him, the dog squeezed out of the family hug, and for a moment, they are as still as death, each holding to each, the sound of the stove fan almost drowning out the voice of Roger Mudd.

The train crosses the marshland. Avery could tell by his nose where he was any step of the way along the railroad bed from Princeton Junction to Penn Station. A jingle came to him: You can tell by the smell that you won't be going to hell. He would have made a good advertising writer and he knew it.

For a reason unknown (as usual), the train stopped, hanging in limbo over the New Jersey flatland. Avery read hard, to keep from worrying about the appointment that he might miss. Biographies, pictures, editorials, remembrances, official statements of grief. This affliction, this teen and tine of the "national spirit" (whatever that was, he thought). It was Russian, almost, or, to bring it

closer, Negro, say—all these expressions of sorrow.
Eat your dinner of horrors, absorb the suffering felt,
but don't build it to a requiem of boohoos. He had
left his wife practically keening on the hassock.
"This will never do," he had said stiffly in that
prudish tone that crept into his voice, always surprising him. The pitch of the puritan headmaster.

I hope she cries like that for me, he thought in a
gesture of jealousy; and then, Go, train, go, goddamn it.

He took out his appointment book (Brooks Brothers, pigskin, gold pencil; a luxury, but what the
hell?). He was late now and Stein already had the
first of his clients. Avery felt sure that Stein was
at this moment offering to buy oils, consider aircraft,
engage mutual funds, sell short, plow into city bonds
and experiment in soybean futures. Stein was becoming for Avery the essence of all the minorities setting
up to threaten him. Minorities! Minorities? There
was no more picked-on minority in the United States
and all its possessions than the white Anglo-Saxon
Protestants. Knock the WASP. Everybody was
doing it. I'm the minority and all the other minorities form the majority; so thought Avery alone
above the wasteland.

Time for another cigarette. He allowed himself
four an hour. Filter-tipped. Hazardous. It said so
right on the pack. See? We all run risks. Some are
more dramatic than others. That's the only difference. Inhales deeply, holds it, exhales in a sigh,
belches quietly.

It was this feeling of being cheated that churned
his stomach acids. Cheated in this particular instance
by the railroad that had promised to deliver him from
one given point to another in a certain time period.
Today this was not happening. Cheated in a grander
sense by all the irresponsible people who got in his
way, cut into line, ignored rules, undercut, undersold,
outyelled, muscled past, tripped on his heels. Cheated

further by his own bosses and potentates, who liked him and congratulated him and predicted great things for him but seldom seemed to really know him. And this on top of the fact that Avery did almost everything right.

Take, for example, the common view in Avery's world of the lately slain late-beloved-by-some. The man was, among other things, a troublemaker, a stirrer upper, a tax-loophole closer and a nigger lover. He was long-haired and a friend of the long-hairs. It was difficult to find a business leader (Avery was liberal; he would add labor leader) who backed the man politically. And yet, and yet, sensing that the attacks in the trade magazines had been too strong, and aware that no one was totally bad, Avery had defended the kid only three days ago at a business luncheon. At the time, he had wondered if his pose of sweet reason would offend his superiors, and at the time, perhaps it did. But now, only a few hours later in terms of life lived, the deed had been done and there was some shared sense of guilt and Avery hoped, in the back of his mind, that his own defense of the candidate would be remembered now.

In the strangely empty car that rocked occasionally in the wind, Avery read the clothing ads, the market reports, the shipping schedules, the weather map, times and names of satellites, the sports page and, having nothing else to do, he reread the exequies and obits in three other newspapers—Washington, Trenton and a New York rag.

Thank God for the air conditioning, he thought along about noontime; if I have to wait here much longer, I'll get out and walk. Having muttered that, he immediately regretted it. Not only was it unsafe, it provoked the terrible image he had often grappled with, that claustrophobic conception of trying desperately in some crisis or other to make his way under the river, through the train tunnel, flattening his body against the dirty, damp walls each time a

train roared through, hoping that by making himself
thin and curved, he would not be cut in half by an
open door or dragged under the wheels to be buffeted and cut into pulp. Subways brought this picture
to him, too. No, he would not get out and walk.
Better to stay put and let the railroad take care of
him.

He did three crossword puzzles (finding, by coinci-
dence, *pariah dog* used in all three of them). In a
fit of humor and rebellion, he drew mustaches on
the pictures of the debutantes. He tore out a theater
review of a play that would interest one of the sec-
retaries at work. He crumpled various pages of the
want ads and molded them into balls, which he
tossed up at the coatrack, but he tired of this game,
because he could dunk a shot without rising from
his seat.

Along about three o'clock, his concern was evi-
denced by his frequent use of the toilet. This was a
car with a small room marked LADIES, and Avery
would not have violated any principles except he
was bursting, his teeth almost floating, and there was
no one else in the car. Just to be certain, he locked
the door carefully behind himself each time he entered the territory and he sang while he urinated,
to advertise his presence.

In his spare time, he outlined his argument for
the continuation of the oil-depletion allowance. His
rage, his fury, his impatience with all things not in
homeostasis poured into his note-taking and he
found himself losing control, talking out loud, kicking at the seat in front of him. He jabbed his pencil
at the paper time and time again and discovered
that he had piled through to his leg, puncturing his
thigh with tiny blood marks. Now angry at ruining
his suit, he limped up and down the aisle and gave
a lecture against the ghetto riots that were destroying
the cities he didn't live in.

His training, his education, his self-control soon

came back to him and he returned to his seat to
take a nap (he had actually spread out, placing his
newspapers in the seats across the aisle).

It was just past five o'clock, thereabouts, when he
woke. Stein had all his business now, he figured.
The sun was still strong but sinking. For the first
time, Avery realized that no other trains had been
by all day. The intense quiet, the buzzing silence,
soothed him. He yawned. A gentle throbbing of the
right mastoid bone made him fidget. An aspirin would
have helped, a drink even more. But let that pass.

Bored, and with what he took to be an artistic
urge for a view, he raised his window shade to
study the New York skyline. It wasn't there. Confused only for a moment, Avery slowly raised the
shade opposite to look at Newark. It wasn't there,
either. The Turnpike rose on its tall columns, but
Avery could see no traffic of any kind. It did not
seem foggy, but Avery supposed that fog was the
reason his vision was blocked. Or perhaps clouds—
although fog is clouds; that's right, he'd forgotten
that.

Anyway, he thought as he returned to his seat and
folded a sheet of newspaper into a complicated
pattern that, when cut properly and opened, would
spring into an artificial Christmas tree, anyway, it's
a hell of a way to run a railroad.

Leave him there, hanging there, no journey completed, full-circleless, stewing in his own juices,
plumped with his beliefs, ready for whatever.

Leviathan!

larry niven

Two men stood on one side of a thick glass wall.
"You'll be airborne," Svetz's beefy, red-faced boss
was saying. "We made some improvements in the
small extension cage while you were in the hospital.
You can hover it or fly it at up to fifty miles per
hour or let it fly itself; there's a constant-altitude
setting. Your field of vision is total. We've made
the shell of the extension cage completely transparent."

On the other side of the thick glass, something
was trying to kill them. It was 40 feet long from
nose to tail and was equipped with vestigial batlike
wings. Otherwise, it was built something like a slender lizard. It screamed and scratched at the glass
with murderous claws.

The sign on the glass read:

GILA MONSTER
RETRIEVED FROM THE YEAR 230 ANTE-ATOMIC,
APPROXIMATELY, FROM THE REGION OF CHINA,
EARTH. EXTINCT.

"You'll be well out of his reach," said Ra Chen.
"Yes, sir." Svetz stood with his arms folded about
him, as if he had a chill. He was being sent after

the biggest animal that had ever lived, and Svetz was afraid of animals.

"For science's sake! What are you worried about, Svetz? It's only a big fish!"

"Yes, sir. You said that about the Gila monster. It's just an extinct lizard, you said."

"We had only a drawing in a children's book to go by. How could we know it would be so big?"

The Gila monster drew back from the glass. It inhaled hugely and took aim. Yellow-and-orange flame spewed from its nostrils and played across the glass. Svetz squeaked and jumped for cover.

"He can't get through," said Ra Chen.

Svetz picked himself up. He was a slender, small-boned man with pale skin, light-blue eyes and very fine ash-blond hair. "How could we know it would breathe fire?" he mimicked. "That lizard almost *cremated* me. I spent four months in the hospital as it was. And what really burns me is, he looks less like the drawing every time I see him. Sometimes I wonder if I didn't get the wrong animal."

"What's the difference, Svetz? The secretary-general loved him. That's what counts."

"Yes, sir. Speaking of the secretary-general, what does he want with a sperm whale? He's got a horse, he's got a Gila monster——"

"That's a little complicated." Ra Chen grimaced. "Palace politics! It's *always* complicated. Right now, Svetz, somewhere in the United Nations palace, a hundred different scientists are trying to get support, each for his own project. And every last one of them involves getting the attention of the secretary-general and *holding* it. Keeping his attention isn't easy."

Svetz nodded. Everybody knew about the secretary-general.

The family that had ruled the United Nations for 700 years was somewhat inbred.

The secretary-general was 44 years old. He was a happy person; he loved animals and flowers and pictures and people. Pictures of planets and multiple-star systems made him clap his hands and coo with delight; so the Institute for Space Research shared amply in the United Nations budget. But he liked extinct animals, too.

"Someone managed to convince the secretary-general that he wants the largest animal on earth. The idea may have been to take us down a peg or two," said Ra Chen. "Someone may think we're getting too big a share of the budget.

"By the time I got onto it, the secretary-general wanted a Brontosaurus. We'd never have gotten him that. No extension cage will reach that far."

"Was it your idea to get him a whale, sir?"

"Yeah. It wasn't easy to persuade him. Whales have been extinct for so long that we don't even have pictures. All I had to show him was a crystal sculpture from Archaeology—dug out of the Steuben Glass building—and a Bible and a dictionary. I managed to convince him that Leviathan and the sperm whale were one and the same."

"That's not strictly true." Svetz had read a computer-produced condensation of the Bible. The condensation had ruined the plot, in Svetz's opinion. "Leviathan could be anything big and destructive, even a horde of locusts."

"Thank science you weren't there to help, Svetz! The issue was confused enough. Anyway, I promised the secretary-general the largest animal that ever lived on earth. All the literature says that that animal was a whale. And there were sperm-whale herds all over the oceans as recently as the First Century Ante-Atomic. You shouldn't have any trouble finding one."

"In twenty minutes?"

Ra Chen looked startled. "What?"

"If I try to keep the big extension cage in the past for more than twenty minutes, I'll never be able to bring it home. The——"

"I know that."

"—uncertainty factor in the energy constants——"

"Svetz——"

"—will blow the institute right off the map."

"We thought of that, Svetz. You'll go back in the small extension cage. When you find a whale, you'll signal the big extension cage."

"Signal it how?"

"We've found a way to send a simple on-off pulse through time. Let's go back to the institute and I'll show you."

Malevolent golden eyes watched them through the glass as they walked away.

●　●　●

The small extension cage was the part of the time machine that did the moving. Within its transparent shell, Svetz seemed to ride a flying armchair equipped with an airplane passenger's lunch tray, except that the lunch tray was covered with lights and buttons and knobs and crawling green lines. He was somewhere off the east coast of North America, in or around the year 100 Ante-Atomic, or 1845 Anno Domini. The temporal-precession gauge was not particularly accurate.

Svetz skimmed low over water the color of lead, beneath a sky the color of slate. But for the rise and fall of the sea, he might almost have been suspended in an enormous sphere painted half light, half dark. He let the extension cage fly itself, 60 feet above the water, while he watched the needle on the NAI, the Nervous Activities Indicator.

Hunting Leviathan.

His stomach was uneasy. Svetz had thought he was adjusting to the peculiar gravitational side effects of time travel. But apparently not.

At least he would not be here long.

On this trip, he was not looking for a mere 40-foot Gila monster. Now he hunted the largest animal that had ever lived. A most conspicuous beast. And now he had a life-seeking instrument, the NAI.

The needle twitched violently.

Was it a whale? But the needle was trembling in apparent indecision. A cluster of sources, then. Svetz looked in the direction indicated.

A clipper ship, winged with white sail, long and slender and graceful as hell. Crowded, too, Svetz guessed. Many humans, closely packed, would affect the NAI in just that manner. A sperm whale—a single center of complex nervous activity—would attract the needle as violently without making it jerk about like that.

The ship would interfere with reception. Svetz turned east and away, but not without regret. The ship was beautiful.

The uneasiness in Svetz's belly was getting worse, not better.

Endless gray-green water rising and falling beneath his flying armchair.

Enlightenment came like something clicking in his head. *Seasick*. On automatic, the extension cage matched its motion to that of the surface over which it flew, and that surface was heaving in great dark swells.

No wonder his stomach was uneasy! Svetz grinned and reached for the manual controls.

The NAI needle suddenly jerked hard over. A bite! thought Svetz, and he looked off to the right. No sign of a ship. And submarines hadn't been invented yet. Had they? No, of course they hadn't.

The needle was rock-steady.

Svetz flipped the call button.

The source of the tremendous NAI signal was off to his right and moving. Svetz turned to follow it. It would be minutes before the call signal reached the Institute for Temporal Research and brought the big extension cage with its weaponry for hooking Leviathan.

• • •

Many years ago, Ra Chen had dreamed of rescuing the library at Alexandria from Caesar's fire. For this purpose, he had built the big extension cage. Its door was a gaping iris, big enough to be loaded while the library was actually burning. Its hold, at a guess, was at least twice large enough to hold all the scrolls in that ancient library.

The big cage had cost a fortune in government money. It had failed to go back beyond 400 A.A., or 1545 A.D. The books burned at Alexandria were still lost to history, or at least to historians.

Such a boondoggle would have broken other men. Somehow, Ra Chen had survived the blow to his reputation.

He had pointed out the changes to Svetz after they returned from the zoo. "We've fitted the cage out with heavy-duty stunners and antigravity beams. You'll operate them by remote control. Be careful not to let the stun beam touch you. It would kill even a sperm whale if you held it on him for more than a few seconds and it'd kill a man instantly. Other than that, you should have no problems."

It was at that moment that Svetz's stomach began to hurt.

"Our major change is the call button. It will actually send us a signal through time, so that we can send the big extension cage back to you. We can land it right beside you, no more than a few minutes off. That took considerable research, Svetz. The treasury raised our budget for this year so that we could get that whale."

Svetz nodded.

"Just be sure you've got a whale before you call for the big extension cage."

Now, 1200 years earlier, Svetz followed an underwater source of nervous impulse. The signal was intensely powerful. It could not be anything smaller than an adult bull sperm whale.

A shadow formed in the air to his right. Svetz watched it take shape: a great gray-blue sphere floating beside him. Around the rim of the door were antigravity beamers and heavy-duty stun guns. The opposite side of the sphere wasn't there; it simply faded away.

To Svetz, that was the most frightening thing about any time machine: the way it seemed to turn a corner that wasn't there.

Svetz was almost over the signal. Now he used the remote controls to swing the antigravity beamers around and down.

He had them locked on the source. He switched them on and dials surged.

Leviathan was *heavy*. More massive than Svetz had expected. He upped the power and watched the NAI needle swing as Leviathan rose invisibly through the water.

Where the surface of the water bulged upward under the attack of the antigravity beams, a shadow formed. Leviathan rising. . . .

Was there something wrong with the shape?

Then a trembling spherical bubble of water rose, shivering, from the ocean, and Leviathan was within it.

Partly within it. He was too big to fit, though he should not have been.

He was four times as massive as a sperm whale should have been and a dozen times as long. He looked nothing like the crystal Steuben sculpture. Leviathan was a kind of serpent, armored with red-bronze scales as big as a viking's shield, armed with teeth like ivory spears. His triangular jaws gaped wide. As he floated toward Svetz, he writhed, seeking with his bulging yellow eyes for whatever strange enemy had subjected him to this indignity.

Svetz was paralyzed with fear and indecision. Neither then nor later did he doubt that what he saw was the Biblical Leviathan. This had to be the largest beast that had ever roamed the sea, a beast large enough and fierce enough to be synonymous with anything big and destructive. Yet—if the crystal sculpture was anything like representational, this was not a sperm whale at all.

In any case, he was far too big for the extension cage.

Indecision stayed his hand—and then Svetz stopped thinking entirely as the great slitted irises found him.

The beast was floating past him. Around its waist was a sphere of weightless water that shrank steadily as gobbets dripped away and rained back to the sea. The beast's nostrils flared—it was obviously an air breather, though not a cetacean.

It stretched, reaching for Svetz with gaping jaws.

Teeth like scores of elephant's tusks all in a row. Polished and needle-sharp. Svetz saw them close about him from above and below, while he sat frozen in fear.

At the last moment, he shut his eyes tight.

When death did not come, Svetz opened his eyes.

The jaws had not entirely closed on Svetz and his armchair. He heard them grinding faintly against— against the invisible surface of the extension cage, whose existence Svetz had forgotten entirely.

Svetz resumed breathing. He would return home with an empty extension cage, to face the wrath of Ra Chen—a fate better than death. He moved his fingers to cut the antigravity beams from the big extension cage.

Metal whined against metal. Svetz whiffed hot oil, while red lights blinked on all over his lunch-tray control board. He hastily turned the beams on again.

The red lights blinked out, one by reluctant one. Through the transparent shell, Svetz could hear

the grinding of teeth. Leviathan was trying to chew
his way into the extension cage.

His released weight had nearly torn the cage
loose from the rest of the time machine. Svetz would
have been stranded in the past, 100 miles out to
sea, in a broken extension cage that probably
wouldn't float, with an angry sea monster waiting to
snap him up. No, he couldn't turn off the antigravity beamers.

But the beamers were on the big extension cage,
and he couldn't hold it more than about 15 minutes
longer. When the big cage was gone, what would
prevent Leviathan from pulling him to his doom?

"I'll stun him off," said Svetz.

There was dark-red palate above him and red gums
and forking tongue beneath, and the long curved
fangs all around. But between the two rows of teeth,
Svetz could see the big extension cage and the battery
of stunners around the door. By eye, he rotated the
stunners until they pointed straight toward Leviathan.

"I must be out of my mind," said Svetz, and he
spun the stunners away from him. He couldn't fire
them at Leviathan without hitting himself.

And Leviathan wouldn't let go.

Trapped.

No, he thought with a burst of relief. He could
escape with his life. The go-home lever would send
his small extension cage out from between the jaws
of Leviathan, back into the time stream, back to the
institute. His mission had failed, but that was hardly
his fault. Why had Ra Chen been unable to uncover
mention of a sea serpent bigger than a sperm whale?

"It's all his fault," said Svetz. And he reached for
the go-home lever. But he stayed his hand.

"I can't just tell him so," he said. For Ra Chen
terrified him.

The grinding of teeth came through the extension
cage.

"Hate to just quit," said Svetz. "Think I'll try something. . . ."

He could see the antigravity beamers by looking between the teeth. He could feel their influence, so nearly were they focused on the extension cage itself. If he focused them just on himself. . . .

He felt the change; he felt both strong and light-headed, like a drunken ballet master. And if he now narrowed the focus. . . .

The monster's teeth seemed to grind harder. Svetz looked between them as best he could.

Leviathan was no longer floating. He was hanging straight down from the extension cage, hanging by his teeth. The antigravity beamers still balanced the pull of his mass, but now they did so by pulling straight up on the extension cage.

The monster was in obvious distress. Naturally. A water beast, he was supporting his own mass for the first time in his life. And by his teeth! His yellow eyes rolled frantically. His tail twitched slightly at the very tip. And still he clung.

"Let go," said Svetz. "Let go, you . . . monster."

The monster's teeth slid, screeching, down the transparent surface, and he fell.

Svetz cut the antigravity a fraction of a second late. He smelled burnt oil and there were tiny red lights blinking off one by one on his lunch-tray control board.

Leviathan hit the water with a sound of thunder. His long, sinuous body rolled over and floated to the surface and lay as if dead. But his tail flicked once and Svetz knew that he was alive.

"I could kill you," said Svetz. "Hold the stunners on you until you're dead. There's time."

But he still had ten minutes to search for a sperm whale. It wasn't time enough. It didn't begin to be time enough, but if he used it all. . . .

The sea serpent flicked its tail and began to swim away. Once, he rolled to look at Svetz and his jaws opened wide in fury. He finished his roll and was fleeing again.

"Just a minute," Svetz said thickly. "Just a science-perverting minute, there." And he swung the stunners to focus.

• • •

Gravity behaved strangely inside an extension cage. While the cage was moving forward in time, *down* was all directions outward from the center of the cage. Svetz was plastered against the curved wall. He waited for the trip to end.

Seasickness was nothing compared with the motion sickness of time travel.

Free fall, then normal gravity. Svetz moved unsteadily to the door.

Ra Chen was waiting to help him out. "Did you get it?"

"Leviathan? No, sir." Svetz looked past his boss. "Where's the big extension cage?"

"We're bringing it back slowly to minimize the gravitational side effects. But if you don't have the whale——"

"I said I don't have Leviathan."

"Well, just what *do* you have?" Ra Chen demanded.

Somewhat later, he said, "It wasn't?"

Later yet, he said, "You killed him? Why, Svetz? Pure spite?"

"No, sir. It was the most intelligent thing I did during the entire trip."

"But *why?* Never mind, Svetz, here's the big extension cage." A gray-blue shadow congealed in the hollow cradle of the time machine. "And there does seem to be something in it. Hi, you idiots, throw an antigravity beam inside the cage! Do you want the beast crushed?"

The cage had arrived. Ra Chen waved an arm in signal. The door opened.

Something tremendous hovered within the big extension cage. It looked like a malevolent white mountain in there, peering back at its captors with a single tiny, angry eye. It was trying to get at Ra Chen, but it couldn't swim in air.

Its other eye was only a torn socket. One of its flippers was ripped along the trailing edge. Rips and ridges and puckers of scar tissue, and a forest of broken wood and broken steel, marked its tremendous expanse of albino skin. Lines trailed from many of the broken harpoons. High up on one flank, bound to the beast by broken and tangled lines, was the corpse of a bearded man with one leg.

"Hardly in mint condition, is he?" Ra Chen observed.

"Be careful, sir. He's a killer. I saw him ram a sailing ship and sink it clean before I could focus the stunners on him."

"What amazes me is that you found him at all in the time you had left. Svetz, I do not understand your luck. Or am I missing something?"

"It wasn't luck, sir. It was the most intelligent thing I did the entire trip."

"You said that before. About killing Leviathan."

Svetz hurried to explain. "The sea serpent was just leaving the vicinity. I wanted to kill him, but I knew I didn't have the time. I was about to leave, myself, when he turned back and bared his teeth.

"He was an obvious carnivore. Those teeth were built strictly for killing, sir. I should have noticed earlier. And I could think of only one animal big enough to feed a carnivore that size."

"Ahhh. Brilliant, Svetz."

"There was corroborative evidence. Our research never found any mention of giant sea serpents. The great geological surveys of the First Century Post-Atomic should have turned up something. Why didn't they?"

"Because the sea serpent quietly died out two

centuries earlier, after whalers killed off his food supply."

Svetz colored. "Exactly. So I turned the stunners on Leviathan before he could swim away and I kept the stunners on him until the NAI said he was dead. I reasoned that if Leviathan was there, there must be whales in the vicinity."

"And Leviathan's nervous output was masking the signal."

"Sure enough, it was. The moment he was dead, the NAI registered another signal. I followed it to" —Svetz jerked his head. They were floating the whale out of the extension cage—"to him."

• • •

Days later, two men stood on one side of a thick glass wall.

"We took some clones from him, then passed him on to the secretary-general's vivarium," said Ra Chen. "Pity you had to settle for an albino." He waved aside Svetz's protest. "I know, I know, you were pressed for time."

Beyond the glass, the one-eyed whale glared at Svetz through murky sea water. Surgeons had removed most of the harpoons, but scars remained along his flanks; and Svetz, awed, wondered how long the beast had been at war with man. Centuries? How long did sperm whales live?

Ra Chen lowered his voice. "We'd all be in trouble if the secretary-general found out that there was once a bigger animal than this. You understand that, don't you, Svetz?"

"Yes, sir."

"Good." Ra Chen's gaze swept across another glass wall and a fire-breathing Gila monster. Farther down, a horse looked back at him along the dangerous spiral horn in its forehead.

"Always we find the unexpected," said Ra Chen. "Sometimes I wonder. . . ."

If you'd do your research better, Svetz thought. . . .

"Did you know that time travel wasn't even a concept until the First Century Ante-Atomic? A writer invented it. From then until the Fourth Century Post-Atomic, time travel was pure fantasy. It violates everything the scientists thought were natural laws. Logic. Conservation of matter and energy. Momentum, reaction, any law of motion that makes time a part of the statement. Relativity.

"It strikes me," said Ra Chen, "that every time we push an extension cage past that particular five-century period, we shove it into a world that isn't really natural. That's why you keep finding giant sea serpents and fire-breathing——"

"That's nonsense," said Svetz. He was afraid of his boss, yes, but there were limits.

"You're right," Ra Chen said instantly, almost with relief. "Take a month's vacation, Svetz, then back to work. The secretary-general wants a bird."

"A bird?" Svetz smiled. A bird sounded harmless enough. "I suppose he found it in another children's book?"

"That's right. Ever hear of a roc?"

The Monster Show

charles beaumont

"Is it sock?" the big man inquired nervously, flicking a tablet into his mouth.

"It is sock," the official coordinator of TV production replied. "It is wham and boff. I give you my word."

"I give it back to you. Words mean nothing. It's pictures that count. Flap?"

"Sure, flap, flap," the official coordinator said and slipped a small needle into a large vein. "But I tell you, B. P., there is nothing to worry about. We have got thirty cameras regular and sixty in reserve. For every actor, two stand-ins. In fact, we have even got stand-ins for the stand-ins. Nothing can go wrong. Nothing-o."

The big man collapsed into a chair and moved a handkerchief rhythmically across his neck. "I don't know," he said. "I am worried."

"What you should do, B. P.," the official coordinator said, "is, you should relax."

The big man belched a picture off the wall. "Relax!" he shouted. "The most expensive TV production in history and he tells me to relax!"

"B. P., flap this. Everything is scatty-boo. *A* through *Z*. We absotively and posilutely cannot miss."

"I just don't know," the big man said, shaking his head.

The official coordinator removed a red pellet from an onyx case and tossed it into his mouth. "Boss, listen to me for a double-mo. Listen. Close the eyes. Now, you are no longer the chief and commander of production of the world's largest TV studio. . . ."

The big man trembled slightly.

"You are, instead, Mr. Average World Family, 1976 A.D. Flap?"

"Flap, flap."

" 'K. You are sitting in front of your two-thirds-paid-for one-hundred-fifty-inch noncurved wall T-Viewer. You are in your undershirt. The missus has poured you a beer and you are munching Cheese Drackles. Reety-o. Suddenly you see that it is two minutes to eight. You jab the auto-ray and switch channels right away, if you are sucker enough to be on another channel, which, thanks to those lousy feebs at OBC, maybe you are. But not for long! Because for six months you have been hearing about it. The biggest, the greatest, the most spectacular, the *most expensive* production ever to hit the screen. Said I biggest? Said I greatest? Said I most spectacular? Father-o, this is a veritybobble *monster* of a show! So what do we call it? Natcheroony: *The Monster Show!* 'EVERYBODY WILL BE WATCHING IT —WILL YOU?' These words, Mr. Average World Family, are stamped into your brain. You've seen them everywhere: billboards, leaflets, skywriting, magazine ads, the regular fifteen-minute daily commersh, and you've *heard* them everywhere, too: in buses and planes and cars, from your children——"

"Meant to tell you," the big man interrupted, "getting at the children was a good move."

"What about the parrots?"

"The parrots was also a good move."

"I blush, B. P. But hearken-o: There you are. Are you there?"

"Proceed on. I am ears."

" 'K. It is one minute to eight. You are shaking with excitement. Just like all the rest of the folks everywhere else. In the bars, in the theaters, in the homes. Some with ninety-foot curvo screens, some with modest forty-inchers, some even—like the cops and all—with nothing but their wrist-peeps. But they're with ya, you know that. Get the image, B. P.? All over the world, everything stopped, everybody staring at their sets, waiting, waiting. . . ."

"What about the competition?"

The official coordinator stuck his hands in his pockets and did a sort of dance. "B. P., uncle-o—there isn't any!" He grinned widely. "And *that* is my surprise."

The big man opened his eyes. He clutched the arms of the chair. "How's that, how's that?"

"You tell me no stories, I'll tell you no untruths," the official coordinator smirked. "Baby, they have scratched themselves. Us they do not choose to buck. They are offering to the folks in place of their usual maloop a kitty of our own show—which I got a hefty slap for which, mother-o. . . ."

"Now, now," said the big man, smiling slyly, "you did not muscle the OBC boys a little, I hope?"

"Truth-o, uncle. Nay. They plain quit. The eight spot is *ours*!" The official coordinator slapped his hands together. "And who's to blame them? What *The Monster Show* has not got you can mount on the sharp end of an isotope. Flap this: We begin with a two-hour commercial roundup, advertising the products of our fifty-seven sponsors: General Turbines, Sleep-Neat Capsules, Chewey-Flakes, the Komfy-Kool TV Furniture line and ek cetera. But are these ordinary commershes? Noo. We have them tricked out so they look prezactly like the show. Excavate?"

"Yo."

" 'K. Then, into the show. And *what* a show! I ask you, Mr. Average World Family, at night when you're all blasted out and ready for the old air matt, do you like to get spooned a lot of maloop you have got to *think* about, or do you like to get *round*?"

The big man made a solemn circle with his finger.

"And what is the roundest? Something long and complex and all drawn out? Nay. *Variety*—that's what is the roundest. So we give you a variety show. Starting things off with a kronch, we have a half-hour trained-dog act. Then right into fifteen minutes of old western-movie footage, with the middle reel of a British mystery for the capper. Then a full hour of wrestling, male and female. Ears?"

"Ears."

"A mere starteroo, B. P. We punch 'em with twenty minutes of hillbilly-style used-car commersh, and then we *really* start fighting. A right cross with Reverend Vincent Bell on *How to Live Up to the Hilt*; a left jab with the first installment of a new detergent opera, *Jill Jackson, Jet Wife;* an uppercut to the jaw with *Who's Zoo*—keep moving; don't give 'em a chance to think, see—followed by a flurry of lightning blows to the face and body: *Chef Gaston Escargot's School of Cookery*! *Mike Tometrist, Private Op*! *A Ten-Year Roundup of Stock Turbo and Jalopy Racing*! A musical remake of the old motion picture *Waterloo Bridge*, now called *London Derrière*!" The official coordinator was warming to his topic; his eyes were wide and his lower lip moist. "Do we swing?"

The big man nodded. "Speaking as Mr. Average World Family," he said, "I am getting slightly interested. Wing on."

"Well, we got 'em dizzy now, flap? 'K. We ease off with a hand-cream commersh—you know, the voodoo-dance routine? Thirty minutes. Then, quos! Right in the old schwanzola!"

"What do we do, what do we do?" the big man asked.

"We let 'em have it. POW!" The official coordinator needled a vein ecstatically and exploded, "The old haymaker. The slamboreeno. *Twenty* of the world's greatest comedians on stage, going through their most famous routines, *all at the same time!*"

There was a pregnant pause.

Then the big man shot from his chair, extruded a hirsute hand and laid it gently on the official coordinator's shoulder. "One thing," he said with genuine concern.

"Yes?" the official coordinator quavered.

"Do we have *enough*?"

"B. P., I think we do. I really and truly think we do." The coordinator quickly rolled three pellets into his mouth and grimaced.

"Then," said the big man, "I feel that we ought to be mighty proud. And, flap me, mighty humble, too. Because we are giving the world public the thing they want and need most: *entertainment*." He winked gravely. "Also, we are making for ourselves a few drachmas. Excavate?"

The official coordinator brushed a tear of satisfaction from his cheek. "Boss," he said in cathedral tones, "I promise you this. This I promise you. *Everybody* on earth is going to be watching *The Monster Show* tonight. It is going to be an experience no one will forget. In fact, I will far enough go to say that it will be the most important moment in history!"

The big man squeezed the coordinator's fleshy digits and smiled. "Screech," he said. "You've done poo-goo. Now powder; the mind must rest."

The coordinator nodded, tugged at his forelock and exited through the bulletproof sliding door.

When it was firmly shut, the big man went over and locked it; then he removed from his pocket a flat disk with three knobs. He twiddled the knobs.

There was a humming.

"As planned," the big man said and put the triple-knobbed disk back into his pocket.

His face was curiously devoid of expression. There was perhaps a trace of amusement about the mouth ends as he went to the chromium bar and poured himself a shot of amber; perhaps not. He tilted the glass, swallowed, hiccuped, set the glass down and punched the interoffice audio box. "Miss Dovecoat," he said, "please flap me good. I will see no one between now and the show. Out?"

"And over," the voice of Miss Dovecoat crackled.

The big man sat in the chair, silent and unmoving, expressionless as a barracuda, for four and a half hours.

At ten minutes to eight, he pressed 17 levers on his desk and listened to 17 *yessirs*.

"Report?" he barked.

"Scatoreeny, sir," came the answer like a celestial choir somewhat off-key.

"Sure?"

"Absotive and posilute."

"Everything moving?"

"With an *O*. With a *K*."

"Unbad, gentlemen."

"You snap the whip, we'll take the voyage."

"Ears out, now. *Coverage*?"

"One hundred percent."

"One hundred percent?"

"One hundred per*cent*!"

" 'K. Gentlemen, proceed on."

The big man turned off all the levers and touched a concealed desk button. The three walls of the room seemed to shimmer and reshape themselves into a perfect curve; then they became clear. The image of a man 50 feet tall appeared. He was smiling and pouring a hundred gallons of beer into a gigantic glass.

"*. . . so get those taste buds unlimbered, folksies,*

and treat yourselves to the world's favorite brew: Rocky Mountain! Yes! That's absotively right! I said Rocky Mountain! And. . . ."

In moments the giant man faded and there was a portentous pause.

Then, the sound of a thousand trumpets and an aerial shot of 70 hand-picked chorus girls, so arranged as to spell out:

THE
MONSTER
SHOW

The big man waited a moment, until the emcee had come onstage; then he snapped the concealed button and the walls became walls again.

He removed the triple-knobbed disk. "Now," he said and slumped into a chair.

Hours passed, but he did not move.

Finally, there was a sharp knock at the bullet-proof sliding door.

The big man went to the door and opened it cautiously. Eight lavender creatures with slimy skin and no noses at all were at the threshold.

"Well?" the big man said. "How did it go?"

One of the creatures, slightly more lavender than the rest, stepped forward. "Extremely well," it said. "In fact, perfectly. The Earth people are all dead. Thanks, Volshak, to you."

"Nonsense," the big man said, turning into a lavender creature with slimy skin and no nose at all. "I have had quite enough idolatry. I prefer to think of myself merely as an agent who tried to do his job."

"Volshak, Volshak," the creature hissed, "such modesty is touching and a credit to our race, but there is no getting around it—you are a hero. Why, if there had been the slightest resistance, we would have failed. We had few weapons, a bare handful of warriors—frankly, we were very nearly ready to descend into the great abyss. But even the gulfs are full of vanquished invaders; we did not have, so to speak, a pit to pass in. But now we may revel in the sunlight and enjoy the blessings of propagation on a new world without having lost a single thrimp." The creature put a boneless tentacle forward. "How did you manage it? Volshak, *how* did you manage to put *all* the Earth people to sleep at the same time?"

But Volshak was blushing. He turned his unproboscidean face to the wall and muttered in a small, proud voice, "It was easy."

The Illustrated Woman

ray bradbury

When a new patient wanders into the office and stretches out to stutter forth a compendious ticker tape of free association, it is up to the psychiatrist immediately beyond, behind and above to decide at just which points of the anatomy the client is in touch with the couch.

In other words, where does the patient make contact with reality?

Some people seem to float half an inch above any surface whatsoever. They have not seen earth in so long they have become somewhat airsick.

Still others so firmly weight themselves down, clutch, thrust, heave their bodies toward reality that long after they are gone you find their tiger shapes and claw marks in the upholstery.

In the case of Emma Fleet, Dr. William C. George was a long time deciding which was furniture and which was woman and where what touched which.

For, to begin with, Emma Fleet resembled a couch.

"Mrs. Emma Fleet, Doctor," announced his receptionist.

Dr. William C. George gasped.

And it *was* a traumatic experience, seeing this

38

woman shunt herself through the door without benefit of railroad switchman or the ground crews who rush about under Macy's Easter balloons, heaving on lines, guiding the massive images to some eternal hangar off beyond.

In came Emma Fleet, as quick as her name, the floor shifting like a huge scale under her weight.

Dr. George must have gasped again, guessing her at 400 on the hoof, for Emma Fleet smiled as if reading his mind.

"Four hundred and two and one-half pounds, to be exact," she said.

He found himself staring at his furniture.

"Oh, it'll hold all right," said Mrs. Fleet intuitively.

She sat down.

The couch yelped like a cur.

Dr. George cleared his throat. "Before you make yourself comfortable," he said, "I feel I should say immediately and honestly that we in the psychiatric field have had little success in inhibiting appetites. The whole problem of weight and food has so far eluded our ability for coping. A strange admission, perhaps, but unless we put our frailties forth, we might be in danger of fooling ourselves and thus taking money under false pretenses. So, if you are here seeking help for your figure, I must list myself among the nonplused."

"Thank you for your honesty, Doctor," said Emma Fleet. "However, I don't wish to lose. I'd prefer your helping me *gain* another one hundred or two hundred pounds."

"Oh, no!" Dr. George exclaimed.

"Oh, yes. But my heart will not allow what my deep dear soul would most gladly endure. My physical heart might fail at what my loving heart and mind would ask of it."

She sighed. The couch sighed.

"Let me brief you. I'm married to Willy Fleet.

We work for the Dillbeck-Hornemann Traveling Shows. I'm known as Lady Bountiful. And, Willy . . .?"

She swooned up out of the couch and glided, or rather escorted, her shadow across the floor. She opened the door.

Beyond, in the waiting room, a cane in one hand, a straw hat in the other, seated rigidly, staring at the wall, was a tiny man with tiny feet and tiny hands and tiny bright blue eyes in a tiny head. He was, at the most, one would guess, three feet high and probably weighed 60 pounds in the rain. But there was a proud, gloomy, almost violent look of genius blazing in that small but craggy face.

"That's Willy Fleet," said Emma lovingly and shut the door.

The couch, sat on, cried again.

Emma beamed at the psychiatrist, who was still staring, in shock, at the door.

"No children, of course?" he heard himself say.

"No children." Her smile lingered. "But that's not my problem, either. Willy, in a way, is my child. And I, in a way, besides being his wife, am his mother. It all has to do with size, I imagine, and we're happy with the way we've balanced things off."

"Well, if your problem isn't children, or your size or his, or controlling weight, then what . . . ?"

Emma Fleet laughed lightly, tolerantly. It was a nice laugh, like a girl's somehow caught in that great body and throat.

"Patience, Doctor. Mustn't we go back down the road to where Willy and I first met?"

The doctor shrugged, laughed quietly himself and relaxed, nodding. "You must."

"During high school," said Emma Fleet, "I weighed one-eighty and tipped the scales at two-fifty when I was twenty-one. Needless to say, I went on few summer excursions. Most of the time I was left in dry dock. I had many girlfriends, however, who liked to be seen with me. They weighed one-fifty, most of them, and I made them feel svelte. But . . . that's a long time ago. I don't worry over it anymore. Willy changed all that."

"Willy sounds like a remarkable man," Dr. George found himself saying, against all the rules.

"Oh, he is, he is! He—*smolders*—with ability, with talent as yet undiscovered, untapped!" she said, quickening warmly. "God bless him, he leaped into my life like summer lightning! Eight years ago I went with my girlfriends to the visiting Labor Day carnival. By the end of the evening, the girls had all been seized away from me by the running boys who, rushing by, grabbed and took them off into the night. There I was alone with three Kewpie dolls, a fake alligator handbag and nothing to do but make the GUESS YOUR WEIGHT man nervous by looking at him every time I went by and pretending like at any moment I might pay my money and dare him to guess.

"But the GUESS YOUR WEIGHT man *wasn't* nervous! After I had passed three times, I saw him staring at me. With awe, yes, with admiration! And who was this GUESS YOUR WEIGHT man? Willy Fleet, of course. The fourth time I passed he called to me and said I could get a prize free if only I'd let him guess my weight. He was all feverish and excited. He danced around. I'd never been made over so much in my life. I blushed. I felt good. So I sat in the scales chair. I heard the pointer whizz around and I heard Willy whistle with honest delight.

" 'Two hundred and eighty-nine pounds!' he cried. 'Oh, boy, oh, boy, you're *lovely*!'

" 'I'm *what*?' I said.

" 'You're the loveliest woman in the whole world,' said Willy, looking me right in the eye.

"I blushed again. I laughed. We both laughed. Then I must have cried, for the next thing, sitting there, I felt him touch my elbow with concern. He was gazing into my face, faintly alarmed.

" 'I haven't said the wrong thing . . . ?' he asked.

" 'No,' I sobbed and then grew quiet. 'The right thing, only the right thing. It's the first time anyone ever——'

" 'What?' he said.

" 'Ever put up with my fat,' I said.

" 'You're not fat,' he said. 'You're large, you're big, you're wonderful. Michelangelo would have loved you. Titian would have loved you. Da Vinci would have loved you. They knew what they were doing in those days. Size. Size is everything. I should know. Look at me. I traveled with Singer's Midgets for six seasons, known as Jack Thimble. And, oh, my God, dear lady, you're right out of the most glorious part of the Renaissance. Bernini, who built those colonnades around the front of St. Peter's and inside at the altar, would have sold his everlasting soul just to know someone like you. . . .'

" 'Don't!' I cried. 'I wasn't meant to feel this happy. It'll hurt so much when you stop.'

" 'I won't stop, then,' he said. 'Miss . . . ?'

" 'Emma Gertz.'

" 'Emma,' he said, 'are you married?'

" 'Are you kidding?' I said.

" 'Emma, do you like to travel?'

" 'I've never traveled.'

" 'Emma,' he said, 'this old carnival's going to be in your town one more week. Come down every night, every day, why not? Talk to me, know me. At the end of the week, who can tell, maybe you'll travel with me.'

" 'What are you suggesting?' I said, not really angry or irritated or anything, but fascinated and intrigued that anyone would offer anything to Moby Dick's daughter.

" 'I mean marriage!' Willy Fleet looked at me, breathing hard, and I had the feeling that he was dressed in a mountaineer's rig, alpine hat, climbing boots, spikes, and a rope slung over his baby shoulder. And if I should ask him, 'Why are you saying this?' he might well answer, 'Because you're *there.*'

"But I didn't ask, so he didn't answer. We stood there in the night, at the center of the carnival, until at last I started off down the midway, swaying. 'I'm drunk!' I cried. 'Oh, so very drunk, and I've had nothing to drink.'

" 'Now that I've found you,' called Willy Fleet after me, 'you'll never escape me, remember!'

"Stunned and reeling, blinded by his large man's words sung out in his soprano voice, I somehow blundered from the carnival grounds and trekked home.

"The next week, we were married."

Emma Fleet paused and looked at her hands.

"Would it bother you if I told about the honeymoon?" she asked shyly.

"No," said the doctor, then lowered his voice, for he was responding all too quickly to the details. "Please *do* go on."

"The honeymoon." Emma sounded her *vox humana*. The response from all the chambers of her body vibrated the couch, the room, the doctor, the dear bones within the doctor.

"The honeymoon . . . was not usual."

The doctor's eyebrows lifted the faintest touch. He looked from the woman to the door beyond which, in miniature, sat the image of Sir Edmund Hillary, he of Everest.

"You have never seen such a rush as Willy spirited me off to his home, a lovely dollhouse, really, with one large normal-sized room that was to be mine, or rather, ours. There, very politely, always the kind, the thoughtful, the quiet gentleman, he asked for my blouse, which I gave him, my skirt, which I gave him. Right down the list, I handed him the garments that he named, until at last. . . . Can one blush from head to foot? One can. One did. I stood like a veritable hearth fire stoked by a blush of all-encompassing and ever-moving color that surged and resurged up and down my body in tints of pink and rose and then pink again.

" 'My God!' cried Willy. 'You're the loveliest grand camellia that ever did unfurl!' Whereupon new tides of blush moved in hidden avalanches within, showing only to color the tent of my body, the outermost and, to Willy, anyway, most precious skin.

"What did Willy do then? Guess."

"I daren't," said the doctor, flustered himself.

"He walked around and around me."

"*Circled* you?"

"Around and around, like a sculptor gazing at a huge block of snow-white granite. He said so himself. Granite or marble from which he might shape images of beauty as yet unguessed. Around and around he walked, sighing and shaking his head happily at his fortune, his little hands clasped, his little eyes bright. Where to begin, he seemed to be thinking, where, where to begin!?

"He spoke at last. 'Emma,' he asked, 'why, why do you think I've worked for years as the GUESS YOUR WEIGHT man at the carnival? Why? Because I have been searching my lifetime through for such as you. Night after night, summer after summer, I've watched those scales jump and twitter! And now at last I've the means, the way, the wall, the canvas, whereby to express my genius!'

"He stopped walking and looked at me, his eyes brimming over.

" 'Emma,' he said softly, 'may I have permission to do anything absolutely whatsoever at all with you?'

" 'Oh, Willy, Willy,' I cried. 'Anything!' "

Emma Fleet paused.

The doctor found himself out at the edge of his chair.

"Yes, yes. And *then?*"

"And then," said Emma Fleet, "he brought out all his boxes and bottles of inks and stencils and his bright silver tattoo needles."

"Tattoo needles?"

The doctor fell back in his chair.

"He . . . tattooed you?"

"He tattooed me."

"He was a tattoo artist?"

"He was, he is, an artist. It only happens that the form his art takes happens to be the tattoo."

"And you," said the doctor slowly, "were the canvas for which he had been searching much of his adult life?"

"I was the canvas for which he had searched *all* of his adult life."

She let it sink, and it *did* sink, and kept on sinking, into the doctor. Then when she saw it had struck bottom and stirred up vast quantities of mud, she went serenely on.

"So our grand life began! I loved Willy and Willy loved me and we both loved this thing that was larger than ourselves that we were doing together. Nothing less than creating the greatest picture the world has ever seen! 'Nothing less than perfection!' cried Willy. 'Nothing less than perfection!' cried myself, in response.

"Oh, it was a happy time. Ten thousand cozy, busy hours we spent together. You can't imagine how proud it made me to be the vast shore along which the genius of Willy Fleet ebbed and flowed in a tide of colors.

"One year alone we spent on my right arm and my left, half a year on my right leg, eight months on my left, in preparation for the grand explosion of bright detail which erupted out along my collarbones and shoulder blades, which fountained upward from my hips to meet in a glorious July celebration of pinwheels, Titian nudes, Giorgione landscapes and El Greco cross-indexes of lightning on my façade, prickling with vast electric fires up and down my spine.

"Dear me, there never has been, there never will be, a love like ours again, a love where two people so sincerely dedicated themselves to one task, of giving beauty to the world in equal portions. We flew to each other day after day, and if I ate more, grew larger with the years, Willy approved, Willy applauded. Just that much more room, more space, for his configurations to flower in. We could not bear to be apart, for we both felt, were certain, that once the Masterpiece was finished, we could leave circus, carnival or vaudeville forever. It was grandiose, yes, but we knew that once finished, I could be toured through the Art Institute in Chicago, the Kress Collection in Washington, the Tate Gallery in London, the Louvre, the Uffizi, the Vatican Museum! For the rest of our lives we would travel with the sun!

"So it went, year on year. We didn't need the world or the people of the world; we had each other. We worked at our ordinary jobs by day, and then till after midnight, there was Willy at my ankle, there was Willy at my elbow, there was Willy exploring up the incredible slope of my back toward the snowy-talcumed crest. Willy wouldn't let me see most of the time. He didn't like me looking over his shoulder; he didn't like me looking over *my* shoulder, for that matter. Months passed before, curious beyond madness, I would be allowed to see his progress, slow inch by inch, as the brilliant inks inundated me and I drowned in the rainbow of his inspirations. Eight years, eight glorious, wondrous years. And then at last, it was done, it was finished. And Willy threw himself down and slept for forty-eight hours straight. And I slept near him, the mammoth bedded with the black lamb. That was just four weeks ago. Four short weeks back, our happiness came to an end."

"Ah, yes," said the doctor. "You and your husband are suffering from the creative equivalent of the 'baby blues,' the depression a mother feels after her child is born. Your work is finished. A listless and somewhat sad period invariably follows. But, now, consider, you will reap the rewards of your long labor, surely? You *will* tour the world?"

"No," cried Emma Fleet, and a tear sprang to her eye. "At any moment, Willy will run off and never return. He has begun to wander about the city. Yesterday I caught him brushing off the carnival scales. Today I found him working, for the first time in eight years, back at his GUESS YOUR WEIGHT booth!"

"Dear me," said the psychiatrist. "He's . . . ?"

"Weighing new women, yes! Shopping for new canvas! He hasn't said, but I know, I know! This time he'll find a heavier woman yet, five hundred, six hundred pounds! I guessed this would happen, a month ago, when we finished the Masterpiece. So I ate still more and stretched my skin still more, so that little places appeared here and there, little open stretches that Willy had to repair, fill in with fresh detail. But now I'm done, exhausted. I've stuffed to distraction; the last fill-in work is done. There's not a millionth of an inch of space left between my ankles and my Adam's apple where he can squeeze in one last demon, dervish or baroque angel. I am, to Willy, work over and done. Now he wants to move on. He will marry, I fear, four more times in his life, each time to a larger woman, a greater extension for a greater mural and the grand finale of his talent. Then, too, in the last week, he has become critical."

"Of the Masterpiece with a capital *M*?" asked the doctor.

"Like all artists, he is a perfectionist. Now he finds little flaws, a face here done slightly in the wrong tint or texture, a hand there twisted slightly askew by my hurried diet to gain more weight and thus give him new space and renew his attentions. To him, above all, I was a beginning. Now he must move on from his apprenticeship to his true masterworks. Oh, Doctor, I am about to be abandoned. Where is there for a woman who weighs four hundred pounds and is laved with illustrations? If he leaves, what shall I do, where go, who would want me now? Will I be lost again in the world as I was lost before my wild happiness?"

"A psychiatrist," said the psychiatrist, "is not supposed to give advice. But——"

"But, but, but?" she cried eagerly.

"A psychiatrist is supposed to let the patient discover and cure himself. Yet, in this case——"

"This case, yes, go on!"

"It seems so simple. To keep your husband's love——"

"To keep his love, yes?"

The doctor smiled. "You must destroy the Masterpiece."

"What?"

"Erase it, get rid of it. Those tattoos *will* come off, won't they? I read somewhere once that——"

"Oh, Doctor!" Emma Fleet leaped up. "That's *it!* It can be done! And best of all, Willy can do it! It will take three months alone to wash me clean, rid me of the very Masterpiece that irks him now. Then, virgin-white again, we can start another eight years, after that another eight and another and another. Oh, Doctor, I know he'll do it! Perhaps he was only waiting for me to suggest—and I too stupid to guess! Oh, Doctor, Doctor!"

And she crushed him in her arms.

When the doctor broke happily free, she stood off, turning in a circle.

"How strange," she said. "In half an hour, you solve the next three thousand days and beyond of my life. You're very wise. I'll pay you anything!"

"My usual modest fee is sufficient," said the doctor.

"I can hardly wait to tell Willy! But first," she said, "since you've been so wise, you deserve to see the Masterpiece before it is destroyed."

"That's hardly necessary, Mrs.——"

"You must discover for yourself the rare mind, eye and artistic hand of Willy Fleet, before it is gone forever and we start anew!" she cried, unbuttoning her voluminous frock coat.

"It isn't really——"

"There!" she said and flung her coat wide.

The doctor was somehow not surprised to see that she was stark-naked beneath her coat.

He gasped. His eyes grew large. His mouth fell open. He sat down slowly, though in reality he somehow wished to stand, as he had in the fifth grade as a boy, during the salute to the flag, following which three dozen voices broke into an awed and tremulous song:

> *"O beautiful for spacious skies,*
> *For amber waves of grain,*
> *For purple mountain majesties,*
> *Above the fruited plain. . . ."*

But, still seated, overwhelmed, he gazed at the continental vastness of the woman.

Upon which nothing whatsoever was stitched, painted, water-colored or in any way tattooed.

Naked, unadorned, untouched, unlined, unillustrated.

He gasped again.

Now she had whipped her coat back about her with a winsome acrobat's smile, as if she had just performed a towering feat. Now she was sailing toward the door.

"Wait——" said the doctor.

But she was out the door, in the reception room, babbling, whispering, "Willy, Willy!" and bending to her husband, hissing in his tiny ear until *his* eyes flexed wide, and his firm and passionate mouth dropped open and he cried aloud and clapped his hands with elation.

"Doctor, Doctor, thank you, thank you!"

He darted forward and seized the doctor's hand and shook it hard. The doctor was surprised at the fire and rock hardness of that grip. It was the hand of a dedicated artist, as were the eyes burning up at him darkly from the wildly illuminated face.

"Everything's going to be fine!" cried Willy.

The doctor hesitated, glancing from Willy to the great shadowing balloon that tugged at him wanting to fly off away.

"We won't have to come back again, ever?"

Good Lord, the doctor thought, does *he* think that *he* has illustrated her from stem to stern, and does she humor him about it? Is *he* mad?

Or does *she* imagine that he has tattooed her from neck to toe bone, and does he humor her? Is *she* mad?

Or, most strange of all, do they *both* believe that he has swarmed, as across the Sistine Chapel ceiling, covering her with rare and significant beauties? Do both believe, know, humor each other in their specially dimensioned world?

"Will we have to come back again?" asked Willy Fleet a second time.

"No." The doctor breathed a prayer. "I think not."

Why? Because, by some idiot grace, he had done the right thing, hadn't he? By prescribing for an invisible cause he had made a full cure, yes? Regardless if she believed or he believed or both believed in the Masterpiece, by suggesting the pictures be erased, destroyed, the doctor had made her

a clean, lovely and inviting canvas again, if *she*
needed to be. And if he, on the other hand, wished
a new woman to scribble, scrawl and pretend to
tattoo on, well, that worked, too. For new and
untouched she would be.

"Thank you, Doctor, oh, thank you, thank you!"

"Don't thank me," said the doctor. "I've done
nothing." He almost said, It was all a fluke, a joke, a
surprise! I fell downstairs and landed on my feet!

"Good-bye, good-bye!"

And the elevator slid down, the big woman and
the little man sinking from sight into the now suddenly not too solid earth, where the atoms opened
to let them pass.

"Good-bye, thanks . . . thanks. . . ."

Their voices faded calling his name and praising
his intellect long after they had passed the fourth
floor.

The doctor looked around and moved unsteadily
back into his office. He shut the door and leaned
against it.

"Doctor," he murmured, "heal thyself."

He stepped forward. He did not feel real. He must
lie down, if but for a moment.

Where?

On the couch, of course, on the couch.

The Food of the Gods

arthur c. clarke

It's only fair to warn you, Mr. Chairman, that much of my evidence will be highly nauseating; it involves aspects of human nature that are very seldom discussed in public and certainly not before a congressional committee. But I am afraid that they have to be faced; there are times when the veil of hypocrisy has to be ripped away, and this is one of them.

You and I, gentlemen, have descended from a long line of carnivores. I see from your expressions that most of you don't recognize the term; well, that's not surprising—it comes from a language that has been obsolete for two thousand years. Perhaps I had better avoid euphemisms and be brutally frank, even if I have to use words that are never heard in polite society. I apologize in advance to anyone I may offend.

Until a few centuries ago, the favorite food of almost all men was *meat*—the *flesh* of once-living animals. I'm not trying to turn your stomachs; this is a simple statement of fact, which you can check from any history book——

Why, certainly, Mr. Chairman. I'm quite prepared to wait until Senator Irving feels better. We professionals sometimes forget how laymen may react to statements like that. At the same time, I must warn the committee that there is very much worse to come. If any of you gentlemen are at all squeamish or become easily upset, I suggest you follow the senator before it's too late. . . .

Well, if I may continue. Until modern times, all food fell into two categories. Most of it was produced from plants—cereals, fruits, plankton, algae and other forms of vegetation. It's hard for us to realize that the vast majority of our ancestors have been farmers, winning food from land or sea by primitive and often backbreaking techniques, but that is the truth.

The second type of food, if I may return to this unpleasant subject, was meat, produced from a relatively small number of animals. You may be familiar with some of them—cows, pigs, sheep, whales. Most people—I am sorry to stress this, but the fact is beyond dispute—preferred meat to any other food, though only the wealthiest were able to indulge this appetite. To most of mankind, meat was a rare delicacy in a diet that was more than ninety percent vegetable.

If we look at the matter calmly and dispassionately—as I hope Senator Irving is now in a position to do—we can see that meat was bound to be rare and expensive, for its production is an extremely inefficient process. To make a kilo of meat, the animal concerned had to eat at least ten kilos of vegetable food—very often food that could have been consumed directly by human beings. Quite apart from any consideration of aesthetics, this state of affairs could not be tolerated after the population explosion of the Twentieth Century. Every man who ate meat was condemning ten or more of his fellow humans to starvation. . . .

Luckily for all of us, the biochemists solved the problem; as you may know, the answer was one of the countless by-products of space research. All food —animal or vegetable—is built up from a very few common elements. Carbon, hydrogen, oxygen, nitrogen, traces of sulphur and phosphorous—these half-dozen elements, and a few others, combine in an almost infinite variety of ways to make up every food that man has ever eaten or ever will eat. Faced with the problem of colonizing the Moon and planets, the biochemists of the Twenty-first Century discovered how to synthesize any desired food from the basic raw materials of water, air and rock. It was the greatest, and perhaps the most important, achievement in the history of science, but we should not feel too proud of it. The vegetable kingdom had beaten us by a billion years.

The chemists could now synthesize any conceivable food, whether or not it had a counterpart in nature. Needless to say, there were mistakes—even disasters. Industrial empires rose and crashed; the switch from agriculture and animal husbandry to the giant automatic processing plants and Omniverters of today was often a painful one. But it had to be made, and we are the better for it. The danger of starvation has been banished forever, and we have a richness and variety of food no other age has ever known.

In addition, of course, there was a moral gain. We no longer murder millions of living creatures, and such revolting institutions as the slaughterhouse and the butcher's shop have vanished from the face of the earth. It seems incredible to us that even our ancestors, coarse and brutal though they were, could ever have tolerated such obscenities.

And yet—it is impossible to make a clean break with the past. As I have already remarked, we are carnivores; we inherit tastes and appetites that have been acquired over a million years of time. Whether we like it or not, only a few generations ago our great-grandparents were enjoying the flesh of cattle and sheep and pigs—when they could get it. *And we still enjoy it today.*

Oh, dear, maybe Senator Irving had better stay outside from now onward; perhaps I should not have been quite so blunt. What I meant, of course, was that many of the synthetic foods we now eat have the same formula as the old natural products; some of them, indeed, are such exact replicas that no chemical or other test could reveal any difference. This situation is logical and inevitable; we manufacturers simply took the most popular presynthetic foods as our models and reproduced their taste and texture.

Of course, we also created new names that didn't hint of an anatomical or zoological origin so that no one would be reminded of the facts of life. When you go into a restaurant, most of the words you'll find on the menu have been invented since the beginning of the Twenty-first Century or else adapted from French originals that few people would recognize. If you ever want to find your threshold of tolerance, you can try an interesting but highly unpleasant experiment. The classified section of the Library of Congress has a large number of menus from famous restaurants—yes, and White House banquets—going back for five hundred years. They have a crude, dissecting-room frankness that makes them almost unreadable. I cannot think of anything that reveals more vividly the gulf between us and our ancestors of only a few generations ago.

Yes, Mr. Chairman—I *am* coming to the point; all this is highly relevant, however disagreeable it may be. I am not trying to spoil your appetites; I am merely laying the groundwork for the charge I wish to bring against my competitor, Triplanetary Food Corporation. Unless you understand this background, you may think that this is a frivolous complaint inspired by the admittedly serious losses my firm has sustained since Ambrosia Plus came on the market.

New foods, gentlemen, are invented every week; it is hard to keep track of them. They come and go like women's fashions, and only one in a thousand becomes a permanent addition to the menu. It is *extremely* rare for one to hit the public fancy overnight, and I freely admit that the Ambrosia Plus line of dishes has been the greatest success in the entire history of food manufacture. You all know the position; everything else has been swept off the market.

Naturally, we were forced to accept the challenge. The biochemists of my organization are as good as any in the Solar System, and they promptly got to work on Ambrosia Plus. I am not giving away any trade secrets when I tell you that we have tapes of practically every food, natural or synthetic, that has ever been eaten by mankind—right back to exotic items that you've never heard of, like fried squid, locusts in honey, peacocks' tongues, Venusian polypod. . . . Our enormous library of flavors and textures is our basic stock in trade, as it is with all the firms in the business. From it we can select and mix items in any conceivable combination, and usually we can duplicate, without too much trouble, any product that our competitors put out.

But Ambrosia Plus had us baffled for quite some time. Its protein-fat breakdown classified it as a straightforward meat, without too many complications—yet we couldn't match it exactly. It was the first time my chemists had failed; not one of them could explain just what gave the stuff its extraordinary appeal—which, as we all know, makes every other food seem insipid by comparison. As well it might, but I am getting ahead of myself.

Very shortly, Mr. Chairman, the president of Triplanetary Foods will be appearing before you—rather reluctantly, I'm sure. He will tell you that Ambrosia Plus is synthesized from air, water, limestone, sulphur, phosphorous and the rest. That will be perfectly true, but it will be the least important part of the story. For we have now discovered his secret—which, like most secrets, is very simple once you know it.

I really must congratulate my competitor. He has at last made available unlimited quantities of what is, from the nature of things, the ideal food for mankind. Until now, it has been in extremely short supply, and therefore all the more relished by the few connoisseurs who could obtain it. Without exception, they have sworn that nothing else can remotely compare with it.

Yes, Triplanetary's chemists have done a superb technical job; now *you* have to resolve the moral and philosophical issues. For though it is true that Ambrosia Plus is purely synthetic and has never known the spark of life, it is also true that no scientific test can now distinguish any of us from cannibals.

The Splendid Source

richard matheson

"... Then spare me your slanders, and read
this rather at night than in the daytime, and
give it not to young maidens, if there be any.
... But I fear nothing for this book, since it is
extracted from a high and splendid source,
from which all that has issued has had a great
success...."

—Balzac: *Contes Drolatiques*,
Prologue

It was the one Uncle Lyman told in the summerhouse that did it. Talbert was just coming up the
path when he heard the punch line, " 'My God!'
cried the actress, 'I thought you said *sarsaparilla*!' "

Guffaws exploded in the little house. Talbert
stood motionless, looking through the rose trellis
at the laughing guests. Inside his contour sandals
his toes flexed ruminatively. He thought.

Later he took a walk around Lake Bean and
watched the crystal surf fold over and observed the
gliding swans and stared at the goldfish and thought.

"I've been thinking," he said that night.

"No," said Uncle Lyman haplessly. He did not commit himself further. He waited for the blow.

Which fell.

"Dirty jokes," said Talbert Bean III.

"I beg your pardon?" said Uncle Lyman.

"Endless tides of them covering the nation."

"I fail," said Uncle Lyman, "to grasp the point." Apprehension gripped his voice.

"I find the subject fraught with witchery," said Talbert.

"With——"

"Consider," said Talbert. "Every day, all through our land, men tell off-color jokes: in bars and at ball games, in theater lobbies and at places of business, on street corners and in locker rooms. At home and away, a veritable deluge of jokes."

Talbert paused meaningfully.

"Who makes them up?" he asked.

Uncle Lyman stared at his nephew with the look of a fisherman who has just hooked a sea serpent— half awe, half revulsion.

"I'm afraid——" he began.

"I want to know the source of these jokes," said Talbert, "their genesis, their fountainhead."

"Why?" asked Uncle Lyman weakly.

"Because it is relevant," said Talbert. "Because these jokes are a part of a culture heretofore unplumbed. Because they are an anomaly, a phenomenon ubiquitous yet unknown."

Uncle Lyman did not speak. His pallid hands curled limply on his half-read *Wall Street Journal.* Behind the polished octagons of his glasses, his eyes were suspended berries.

At last he sighed.

"And what part," he inquired sadly, "am I to play in this quest?"

"We must begin," said Talbert, "with the joke you told in the summerhouse this afternoon. Where did you hear it?"

"Kulpritt," Uncle Lyman said. Andrew Kulpritt was one of the battery of lawyers employed by Bean Enterprises.

"Capital," said Talbert. "Call him up and ask him where *he* heard it."

Uncle Lyman drew the silver watch from his pocket.

"It's nearly midnight, Talbert," he announced.

Talbert waved away chronology.

"Now," he said. "This is important."

Uncle Lyman examined his nephew a moment longer. Then, with a capitulating sigh, he reached for one of the Bean mansion's 35 telephones.

Talbert stood toe-flexed on a bearskin rug while Uncle Lyman dialed, waited and spoke.

"Kulpritt?" said Uncle Lyman. "Lyman Bean. Sorry to wake you, but Talbert wants to know where you heard the joke about the actress who thought the director said sarsaparilla."

Uncle Lyman listened. "I *said*——" he began again.

A minute later he cradled the receiver heavily.

"Prentiss," he said.

"Call him up," said Talbert.

"Talbert," Uncle Lyman asked.

"Now," said Talbert.

A long breath exuded between Uncle Lyman's lips. Carefully, he folded his *Wall Street Journal.* He reached across the mahogany table and tamped out his ten-inch cigar. Sliding a weary hand beneath his smoking jacket, he withdrew his tooled-leather address book.

Prentiss heard it from George Sharper, C.P.A. Sharper heard it from Abner Ackerman, M.D. Ackerman heard it from William Cozener, Prune Products. Cozener heard it from Rod Tassell, manager, Cyprian Club. Tassell heard it from O. Winterbottom. Winterbottom heard it from H. Alberts.

Alberts heard it from D. Silver, Silver from B. Phryne, Phryne from E. Kennelly.

By an odd twist, Kennelly said he heard it from Uncle Lyman.

"There is complicity here," said Talbert. "These jokes are not self-generative."

It was four A.M. Uncle Lyman slumped, inert and dead-eyed, on his chair.

"There has to be a source," said Talbert.

Uncle Lyman remained motionless.

"You're not interested," said Talbert incredulously.

Uncle Lyman made a noise.

"I don't understand," said Talbert. "Here is a situation pregnant with diverse fascinations. Is there a man or woman who has never heard an off-color joke? I say not. Yet, is there a man or woman who knows where these jokes come from? Again I say not."

Talbert strode forcefully to his place of musing at the 12-foot fireplace. He poised there, staring in.

"I may be a millionaire," he said, "but I am sensitive." He turned. "And this phenomenon excites me."

Uncle Lyman attempted to sleep while retaining the face of a man awake.

"I have always had more money than I needed," said Talbert. "Capital investment was unnecessary. Thus I turned to investing the other asset my father left—my brain."

Uncle Lyman stirred; a thought shook loose.

"What ever happened," he asked, "to that society of yours, the S.P.C.S.P.C.A.?"

"Eh? The Society for the Prevention of Cruelty to the Society for the Prevention of Cruelty to Animals? The past."

"And your interest in world problems? What about that sociological treatise you were writing . . . ?"

"Slums: A Positive View, you mean?" Talbert brushed it aside. "Inconsequence."

"And isn't there anything left of your political party, the Proantidisestablishmentarianists?"

"Not a shred. Scuttled by reactionaries from within."

"What about bimetallism?"

"Oh, that!" Talbert smiled ruefully. "Passé, dear uncle. I had been reading too many Victorian novels."

"Speaking of novels, what about your literary criticisms? Nothing doing with *The Use of the Semicolon in Jane Austen*? Or *Horatio Alger: The Misunderstood Satirist*? To say nothing of *Was Queen Elizabeth Shakespeare?*"

"*Was Shakespeare Queen Elizabeth?*" corrected Talbert. "No, uncle, nothing doing with them. They had momentary interest, nothing more. . . ."

"I suppose the same holds true for *The Shoehorn: Pro and Con,* eh? And those scientific articles— *Relativity Re-examined* and *Is Evolution Enough?*"

"Dead and gone," said Talbert patiently, "dead and gone. These projects needed me once. Now I go on to better things."

"Like who writes dirty jokes," said Uncle Lyman.

Talbert nodded.

"Like that," he said.

●   ●   ●

When the butler set the breakfast tray on the bed, Talbert said, "Redfield, do you know any jokes?"

Redfield looked out impassively through the face an improvident nature had neglected to animate.

"Jokes, sir?" he inquired.

"You know," said Talbert. "Jollities."

Redfield stood by the bed like a corpse whose casket had been upended and removed.

"Well, sir," he said a full 30 seconds later, "once, when I was a boy, I heard one. . . ."

"Yes?" said Talbert eagerly.

"I believe it went somewhat as follows," Redfield said. "When—uh—*when* is a portmanteau not a——"

"No, no," said Talbert, shaking his head, "I mean *dirty* jokes."

Redfield's eyebrows soared. The vernacular was like a fish in his face.

"You don't know any?" said a disappointed Talbert.

"Begging your pardon, sir," said Redfield, "if I may make a suggestion. May I say that the chauffeur is more likely to——"

"You know any dirty jokes, Harrison?" Talbert asked through the tube as the Rolls-Royce purred along Bean Road toward Highway 27.

Harrison looked blank for a moment. He glanced back at Talbert. Then a grin wrinkled his carnal jowls.

"Well, sir," he began, "there's this guy sittin' by the runway eatin' an onion, see?"

Talbert unclipped his four-color pencil.

• • •

Talbert stood in an elevator rising to the tenth floor of the Gault Building.

The hour's ride to New York had been most illuminating. Not only had he transcribed seven of the most horrendously vulgar jokes he had ever heard in his life but had exacted a promise from Harrison to take him to the various establishments where these jokes had been heard.

The hunt was on.

MAX AXE / DETECTIVE AGENCY, read the words on the frosty-glassed door. Talbert turned the knob and went in.

Announced by the beautiful receptionist, Talbert was ushered into a sparsely furnished office on whose walls were a hunting license, a machine gun and framed photographs of the Seagram factory, the St.

Valentine's Day massacre in color and Herbert J. Philbrick, who had led three lives.

Mr. Axe shook Talbert's hand.

"What could I do for ya?" he asked.

"First of all," said Talbert, "do you know any dirty jokes?"

Recovering, Mr. Axe told Talbert the one about the monkey and the elephant.

Talbert jotted it down. Then he hired the agency to investigate the men Uncle Lyman had phoned and uncover anything that was meaningful.

After he left the agency, Talbert began making the rounds with Harrison. He heard a joke the first place they went.

"There's this midget in a frankfurter suit, see?" it began.

It was a day of buoyant discovery. Talbert heard the joke about the cross-eyed plumber in the harem, the one about the preacher who won an eel at a raffle, the one about the fighter pilot who went down in flames and the one about the two girl scouts who lost their cookies in the laundromat.

Among others.

• • •

"I want," said Talbert, "one round-trip airplane ticket to San Francisco and a reservation at the Hotel Millard Fillmore."

"May I ask," asked Uncle Lyman, "why?"

"While making the rounds with Harrison today," explained Talbert, "a salesman of ladies' undergarments told me that a veritable cornucopia of off-color jokes exists in the person of Harry Shuler, bellboy at the Millard Fillmore. This salesman said that during a three-day convention at that hotel, he had heard more new jokes from Shuler than he had heard in the first thirty-nine years of his life."

"And you are going to——" Uncle Lyman began.

"Exactly," said Talbert. "We must follow where the spoor is strongest."

"Talbert," said Uncle Lyman, "why do you *do* these things?"

"I am searching," said Talbert simply.

"For what, damn it!" cried Uncle Lyman.

"For *meaning*," said Talbert.

Uncle Lyman covered his eyes. "You are the image of your mother," he declared.

"Say nothing of her," charged Talbert. "She was the finest woman who ever trod the earth."

"Then, how come she got trampled to death at the funeral of Rudolph Valentino?" Uncle Lyman charged back.

"That is a base canard," said Talbert, "and you know it. Mother just happened to be passing the church on her way to bringing food to the Orphans of the Dissolute Seamen—one of her many charities —when she was accidentally caught up in the waves of hysterical women and swept to her awful end."

A pregnant silence bellied the vast room. Talbert stood at a window looking down the hill at Lake Bean, which his father had had poured in 1923.

"Think of it," he said after a moment's reflection, "the nation alive with off-color jokes—the *world* alive! And the same jokes, uncle, *the same jokes.* How? *How?* By what strange means do these jokes o'erleap oceans, span continents? By what incredible machinery are these jokes promulgated over mountain and dale?"

He turned and met Uncle Lyman's mesmeric stare.

"I mean to know," he said.

At ten minutes before midnight, Talbert boarded the plane for San Francisco and took a seat by the window. Fifteen minutes later the plane roared down the runway and nosed up into the black sky.

Talbert turned to the man beside him.

"Do you know any dirty jokes, sir?" he inquired, pencil poised.

The man stared at him. Talbert gulped.

"Oh, I *am* sorry," he said, "Reverend."

●   ●   ●

When they reached the room, Talbert gave the bellboy a crisp five-dollar bill and asked to hear a joke.

Shuler told him the one about the man sitting by the runway eating an onion, see? Talbert listened, toes kneading inquisitively in his shoes. The joke concluded, he asked Shuler where this and similar jokes might be overheard. Shuler said at a wharf spot known as Davy Jones's Locker Room.

Early that evening, after drinking with one of the West Coast representatives of Bean Enterprises, Talbert took a taxi to Davy Jones's Locker Room. Entering its dim, smoke-fogged interior, he took a place at the bar, ordered a screwdriver and began to listen.

Within an hour's time he had written down the joke about the old maid who caught her nose in the bathtub faucet, the one about the three traveling salesmen and the farmer's ambidextrous daughter, the one about the nurse who thought they were Spanish olives and the one about the midget in the frankfurter suit. Talbert wrote this last joke under his original transcription of it, underlining changes in context attributable to regional influence.

At 10:16, a man who had just told Talbert the one about the hillbilly twins and their two-headed sister said that Tony, the bartender, was a virtual faucet of off-color jokes, limericks, anecdotes, epigrams and proverbs.

Talbert went over to the bar and asked Tony for the major source of his lewdiana. After reciting the limerick about the sex of the asteroid vermin, the bartender referred Talbert to a Mr. Frank Bruin, salesman, of Oakland, who happened not to be there that night.

Talbert at once retired to a telephone directory, where he discovered five Frank Bruins in Oakland. Entering a booth with a coat pocket sagging change, Talbert began dialing them.

Two of the five Frank Bruins were salesmen. One of them, however, was in Alcatraz at the moment. Talbert traced the remaining Frank Bruin to Hogan's Alleys in Oakland, where his wife said that, as usual on Thursday nights, her husband was bowling with the Moonlight Mattress Company All-Stars.

Quitting the bar, Talbert chartered a taxi and started across the bay to Oakland, toes in ferment.

Veni, vidi, vici?

● ● ●

Bruin was not a needle in a haystack.

The moment Talbert entered Hogan's Alleys his eye was caught by a football huddle of men encircling a portly, rosy-domed speaker. Approaching, Talbert was just in time to hear the punch line followed by an explosion of composite laughter. It was the punch line that intrigued.

" 'My God!' cried the actress," Mr. Bruin had uttered, " 'I thought you said a banana split!' "

This variation much excited Talbert, who saw in it a verification of a new element—the interchangeable kicker.

When the group had broken up and drifted, Talbert accosted Mr. Bruin and, introducing himself, asked where Mr. Bruin had heard that joke.

"Why d'ya ask, boy?" asked Mr. Bruin.

"No reason," said the crafty Talbert.

"I don't remember where I heard it, boy," said Mr. Bruin finally. "Excuse me, will ya?"

Talbert trailed after him but received no satisfaction—unless it was in the most definite impression that Bruin was concealing something.

Later, riding back to the Millard Fillmore, Talbert

decided to put an Oakland detective agency on Mr. Bruin's trail to see what could be seen.

When Talbert reached the hotel, there was a telegram waiting for him at the desk.

> MR. RODNEY TASSELL RECEIVED LONG-DISTANCE CALL FROM MR. GEORGE BULLOCK, CARTHAGE HOTEL, CHICAGO. WAS TOLD JOKE ABOUT MIDGET IN SALAMI SUIT. MEANINGFUL?
> —AXE.

Talbert's eyes ignited.

"Tally," he murmured, *"ho."*

An hour later he had checked out of the Millard Fillmore, taxied to the airport and caught a plane for Chicago.

Twenty minutes after he had left the hotel, a man in a dark pinstripe approached the desk clerk and asked for the room number of Talbert Bean III. When informed of Talbert's departure, the man grew steely-eyed and immediately retired to a telephone booth. He emerged ashen.

* * *

"I'm sorry," said the desk clerk, "Mr. Bullock checked out this morning."

"Oh." Talbert's shoulders sagged. All night on the plane he had been checking over his notes, hoping to discern a pattern to the jokes which would encompass type, area of genesis and periodicity. He was weary with fruitless concentration. Now this.

"And he left no forwarding address?" he asked.

"Only Chicago, sir," said the clerk.

"I see."

Following a bath and luncheon in his room, a slightly refreshed Talbert settled down with the telephone and the directory. There were 47 George Bullocks in Chicago. Talbert checked them off as he phoned.

At three o'clock he slumped over the receiver in

a dead slumber. At 4:21, he regained consciousness and completed the remaining 11 calls. The Mr. Bullock in question was not at home, said his housekeeper, but was expected in that evening.

"Thank you kindly," said a bleary-eyed Talbert and, hanging up, thereupon collapsed on the bed— only to awake a few minutes past seven and dress quickly. Descending to the street, he gulped down a sandwich and a glass of milk, then hailed a cab and made the hour's ride to the home of George Bullock.

The man himself answered the bell.

"Yes?" he asked.

Talbert introduced himself and said he had come to the Carthage Hotel early that afternoon to see him.

"Why?" asked Mr. Bullock.

"So you could tell me where you heard that joke about the midget in the salami suit," said Talbert.

"Sir?"

"I said——"

"I heard what you said, sir," said Mr. Bullock, "though I cannot say that your remark makes any noticeable sense."

"I believe, sir," challenged Talbert, "that you are hiding behind fustian."

"Behind fustian, sir?" retorted Bullock. "I'm afraid——"

"The game is up, sir!" declared Talbert in a ringing voice. "Why don't you admit it and tell me where you got that joke?"

"I have not the remotest conception of what you're talking about, sir!" snapped Bullock, his words belied by the pallor of his face.

Talbert flashed a Mona Lisa smile.

"Indeed?" he said.

And, turning lightly on his heel, he left Bullock trembling in the doorway. As he settled back against the taxicab seat again, he saw Bullock still standing there, staring at him. Then Bullock whirled and was gone.

"Carthage Hotel," said Talbert, satisfied with his bluff.

Riding back, he thought of Bullock's agitation, and a thin smile tipped up the corners of his mouth. No doubt about it. The prey was being run to earth. Now, if his surmise was valid, there would likely be——

A lean man in a raincoat and a derby was sitting on the bed when Talbert entered his room. The man's mustache, like a muddy toothbrush, twitched.

"Talbert Bean?" he asked.

Talbert bowed.

"The same," he said.

The man, a Colonel Bishop, retired, looked at Talbert with metal-blue eyes.

"What is your game, sir?" he asked tautly.

"I don't understand," toyed Talbert.

"I think you do," said the colonel, "and you are to come with me."

"Oh?" said Talbert.

He found himself looking down the barrel of a .45 caliber Webley-Fosbery.

"Shall we?" said the colonel.

"But of course," said Talbert coolly. "I have not come all this way to resist now."

●　●　●

The ride in the private plane was a long one. The windows were blacked out and Talbert hadn't the faintest idea in which direction they were flying. Neither the pilot nor the colonel spoke, and Talbert's attempts at conversation were discouraged by a chilly silence. The colonel's pistol, still leveled at Talbert's chest, never wavered, but it did not bother Talbert. He was exultant. All he could think was that his search was ending; he was at last approaching the headwaters of the dirty joke. After a time, his head nodded and he dozed—to dream of midgets in frankfurter suits and actresses who seemed obsessed by sarsaparilla or banana splits or sometimes both. How long he slept, and what boundaries he may have crossed, Talbert never knew. He was awakened by a swift loss of altitude and the steely voice of Colonel Bishop: "We are landing, Mr. Bean." The colonel's grip tightened on the pistol.

Talbert offered no resistance when his eyes were blindfolded. Feeling the Webley-Fosbery in the small of his back, he stumbled out of the plane and crunched over the ground of a well-kept airstrip. There was a nip in the air and he felt a bit light-headed. Talbert suspected they had landed in a mountainous region, but what mountains, and on what continent, he could not guess. His ears and nose conveyed nothing of help to his churning mind.

He was shoved—none too gently—into an auto-mobile and then driven swiftly along what felt like a dirt road. The tires crackled over pebbles and twigs.

Suddenly the blindfold was removed. Talbert blinked and looked out the windows. It was a black and cloudy night. He could see nothing but the limited vista afforded by the headlights.

"You are well isolated," he said appreciatively. Colonel Bishop remained tight-lipped and vigilant.

After a 15-minute ride along the dark road, the car pulled up in front of a tall, unlighted house. As the motor was cut, Talbert could hear the pulsing rasp of crickets all around.

"Well," he said.

"Emerge," suggested Colonel Bishop.

"Of course." Talbert bent out of the car and was escorted up the wide porch steps by the colonel. Behind, the car pulled away into the night.

Inside the house, chimes bonged hollowly as the colonel pushed a button. They waited in the dark-ness and, in a few moments, approaching footsteps sounded.

A tiny aperture opened in the heavy door, disclosing a single bespectacled eye. The eye blinked once and, with a faint accent Talbert could not recognize, whispered furtively, "Why did the widow wear black garters?"

"In remembrance," said Colonel Bishop with great gravity, "of those who passed beyond."

The door opened.

The owner of the eye was tall, gaunt, of indeterminable age and nationality, his hair a dark mass wisped with gray. His face was all angles and facets, his eyes piercing behind large horn-rimmed glasses. He wore flannel trousers and a checked jacket.

"This is the dean," said Colonel Bishop.

"How do you do," said Talbert.

"Come *in*, come *in*," the dean invited, extending his large hand to Talbert. "Welcome, Mr. Bean." He shafted a scolding look at Bishop's pistol. "Now, Colonel," he said, "indulging in melodramatics again? Put it away, dear fellow, put it away."

"We can't be too careful," grumped the colonel.

Talbert stood in the spacious grace of the entry hall looking around. His gaze settled presently on the cryptic smile of the dean, who said:

"So. You have found us out, sir."

Talbert's toes whipped like pennants in a gale.

"Have I?" he said to cover his excitement.

"Yes," said the dean, "you have. And a masterful display of investigative intuition it was."

Talbert looked around.

"So," he said, voice bated, "it is *here*."

"Yes," said the dean, "would you like to see it?"

"More than anything in the world," said Talbert fervently.

"Come, then," said the dean.

"Is this wise?" the colonel warned.

"Come," repeated the dean.

The three men started down the hallway. For a moment, a shade of premonition darkened Talbert's mind. It was being made so easy. Was it a trap? In a second the thought had slipped away, washed off by a current of excited curiosity.

They started up a winding marble staircase.

"How did you suspect?" the dean inquired. "That is to say—what prompted you to probe the matter?"

"I just *thought*," said Talbert meaningfully, "here are all these jokes; yet no one seems to know where they come from. Or *care*."

"Yes," observed the dean, "we count upon that disinterest. What man in ten million ever asks, Where did you hear that joke? Absorbed in memorizing the joke for future use, he gives no thought to its source. This, of course, is our protection."

The dean smiled at Talbert. "But not," he amended, "from men such as you."

Talbert's flush went unnoticed.

They reached the landing and began walking along a wide corridor lit on each side by the illumination of candelabra. There was no more talk. At the end of the corridor they turned right and stopped in front of massive, iron-hinged doors.

"Is this wise?" the colonel asked again.

"Too late to stop now," said the dean, and Talbert felt a shiver flutter down his spine. What if it *were* a trap? He swallowed, then squared his shoulders. The dean had said it. It was too late to stop now.

The great doors tracked open.

"Et voilà," said the dean.

• • •

The hallway was an avenue. Thick wall-to-wall carpeting sponged beneath Talbert's feet as he walked between the colonel and the dean. At periodic intervals along the ceiling hung music-emitting speakers; Talbert recognized the *Gaieté Parisienne*. His gaze moved to a petit-point tapestry on which Dionysian acts ensued above the stitched motto "Happy Is the Man Who Is Making Something."

"Incredible," he murmured. "Here, in this house."

"Exactly," said the dean.

Talbert shook his head wonderingly.

"To think," he said.

The dean paused before a glass wall and, braking, Talbert peered into an office. Among its rich appointments strode a young man in a striped silk waistcoat with brass buttons, gesturing meaningfully with a long cigar, while cross-legged on a leather couch sat a happily sweatered blonde of rich dimensions.

The man stopped briefly and waved to the dean, smiled, then returned to his spirited dictating.

"One of our best," the dean said.

"But," stammered Talbert, "I thought that man was on the staff of——"

"He is," said the dean. "And, in his spare time, he is also one of us."

Talbert followed on excitement-numbed legs.

"But I had no idea," he said. "I presumed the organization to be composed of men like Bruin and Bullock."

"They are merely our means of promulgation," explained the dean. "Our word-of-mouthers, you might say. Our *creators* come from more exalted ranks—executives, statesmen, the better professional comics, editors, novelists——"

The dean broke off as the door to one of the other offices opened and a barrelly, bearded man in hunting clothes emerged. He shouldered past them muttering true things to himself.

"Off again?" the dean asked pleasantly. The big man grunted. It was a true grunt. He clumped off, lonely for a veld.

"Unbelievable," said Talbert. "Such men as these?"

"Exactly," said the dean.

They strolled on past the rows of busy offices,

Talbert tourist-eyed, the dean smiling his mandarin smile, the colonel working his lips as if anticipating the kiss of a toad.

"But where did it all begin?" a dazed Talbert asked.

"That is history's secret," rejoined the dean, "veiled behind time's opacity. Our venture does have its honored past, however. Great men have graced its cause—Ben Franklin, Mark Twain, Dickens, Swinburne, Rabelais, Balzac; oh, the honor roll is long. Shakespeare, of course, and his friend Ben Jonson. Still further back, Chaucer, Boccaccio. Further yet, Horace and Seneca, Demosthenes and Plautus. Aristophanes, Apuleius. Yea, in the palaces of Tutankhamen was our work done, in the black temples of Ahriman, the pleasure dome of Kublai Khan. Where did it begin? Who knows? Scraped on rock in many a primordial cave are certain drawings. And there are those among us who believe that these were left by the earliest members of the brotherhood. But this, of course, is only legend. . . ."

Now they had reached the end of the hallway and were starting down a cushioned ramp.

"There must be vast sums of money involved in this," said Talbert.

"*Heaven forfend,*" declared the dean, stopping short. "Do not confuse our work with alley vending. Our workers contribute freely of their time and skill, caring for nought save the cause."

"Forgive me," Talbert said. Then, rallying, he asked, "What cause?"

The dean's gaze fused on inward things. He ambled on slowly, arms behind his back.

"The cause of love," he said, "as opposed to hate. Of nature, as opposed to the unnatural. Of humanity, as opposed to inhumanity. Of freedom, as opposed to constraint. Of health, as opposed to disease. Yes, Mr. Bean, disease. The disease called bigotry—the frighteningly communicable disease that taints all it touches, turns warmth to chill and joy to guilt and good to bad. What cause?" He stopped dramatically. "The cause of life, Mr. Bean—as opposed to death!"

The dean lifted a challenging finger. "We see ourselves," he said, "as an army of dedicated warriors marching on the strongholds of prudery. Knights Templar with a just and joyous mission."

"Amen to that," a fervent Talbert said.

They entered a large cubicle-bordered room. Talbert saw men, some typing, some writing, some staring, some on telephones talking in a multitude of tongues. Their expressions were, as one, intently lofty. At the far end of the room, expression unseen, a man stabbed plugs into a many-eyed switchboard.

"Our apprentice room," said the dean, "wherein we groom our future. . . ."

His voice died off as a young man exited one of the cubicles and approached them, paper in hand, a smile tremulous on his lips.

"Oliver," said the dean, nodding once.

"I've done a joke, sir," said Oliver. "May I——"

"But of course," said the dean.

Oliver cleared viscid anxiety from his throat, then told a joke about a little boy and girl watching a doubles match on the nudist-colony tennis court. The dean smiled, nodding. Oliver looked up, pained.

"No?" he said.

"It is not without merit," encouraged the dean, "but, as it now stands, you see, it smacks rather too reminiscently of the duchess-butler effect, *Wife of Bath* category. Not to mention the justifiably popular double-reverse bishop-barmaid gambit."

"Oh, sir," grieved Oliver, "I'll never prevail."

"Nonsense," said the dean, adding kindly, *"son.* These shorter jokes are, by all odds, the most difficult to master. They must be cogent, precise, must say something of pith and moment."

"Yes, sir," murmured Oliver.

"Check with Wojciechowski and Sforzini," said the dean. "Also Ahmed El-Hakim. They'll brief you on use of the master index, eh?" He patted Oliver's back.

"Yes, sir." Oliver managed a smile and returned to his cubicle. The dean sighed.

"A somber business," he declared. "He'll never be class A. He really shouldn't be in the composing end of it at all but"—he gestured meaningfully—"there is sentiment involved."

"Oh?" said Talbert.

"Yes," said the dean. "It was his great-grandfather who, on June 23, 1848, wrote the first traveling-salesman joke, American strain."

The dean and the colonel lowered their heads a moment in reverent commemoration. Talbert did the same.

• • •

"And so we have it," said the dean. They were back downstairs, sitting in the great living room, sherry having been served.

"Perhaps you wish to know more," said the dean.

"Only one thing," said Talbert.

"And that is, sir?"

"Why have you shown it to me?"

"Yes," said the colonel, fingering at his armpit holster, "why indeed?"

The dean looked at Talbert carefully, as if balancing his reply.

"You haven't guessed?" he said at last. "No, I can see you haven't. Mr. Bean . . . you are not unknown to us. Who has not heard of your work, your unflagging devotion to sometimes obscure but always worthy causes? What man can help but admire your selflessness, your dedication, your proud defiance of convention and prejudice?" The dean paused and leaned forward.

"Mr. Bean," he said softly. "Talbert—may I call you that?—*we want you on our team.*"

Talbert gaped. His hands began to tremble. The colonel, relieved, grunted and sank back into his chair.

No reply came from the flustered Talbert; so the dean continued, "Think it over. Consider the merits of our work. With all due modesty, I think I may say that here is your opportunity to ally yourself with the greatest cause of your life."

"I'm speechless," said Talbert. "I hardly—that is—how can I . . . ?"

But, already, the light of consecration was stealing into his eyes.

The Origin of Everything

italo calvino

Through the calculations begun by Edwin P. Hubble on the galaxies' velocity of recession, we can establish the moment when all the universe's matter was concentrated in a single point, before it began to expand.

Naturally, we were all there—*old Qfwfq said*—where else could we have been? Nobody knew then that there could be space. Or time, either: What use did we have for time, packed in there like sardines?

I say packed like sardines, using a literary image; in reality, there wasn't even space to pack us into. Every point of each of us coincided with every point of each of the others in a single point, which was where we all were. In fact, we didn't even bother one another, except for personality differences, because when space doesn't exist, having somebody unpleasant like Mr. Pber^t Pber^d underfoot all the time is the most irritating thing.

How many of us were there? Eh, I was never able to figure that out, not even approximately. To make a count, we would have had to move apart, at least a little; and, instead, we all occupied that same point. Contrary to what you might think, it wasn't the sort

79

of situation that encourages sociability. I know, for example, that in other periods, neighbors called on one another; but there, because of the fact that we were all neighbors, nobody even said good morning or good evening to anybody else.

In the end, each of us associated only with a limited number of acquaintances. The ones I remember most are Mrs. $Ph(i)Nk_0$, her friend De XuaeauX, a family of immigrants by the name of Z'zu and Mr. $Pber^t Pber^d$, whom I just mentioned. There was also a cleaning woman—"maintenance staff," she was called—only one for the whole universe, since there was so little room. To tell the truth, she had nothing to do all day long, not even dusting—inside one point not even a grain of dust can enter—so she spent all her time gossiping and complaining.

Just with the people I've already named, we would have been overcrowded, but you have to add all the stuff we had to keep piled up in there: all the material that was to serve afterward to form the universe, now dismantled and concentrated in such a way that you weren't able to tell what was later to become part of astronomy (like the nebula of Andromeda) from what was assigned to geography (the Vosges, for example) or to chemistry (like certain beryllium isotopes). And on top of that, we were always bumping against the Z'zu family's household goods: camp beds, mattresses, baskets; these Z'zus, if you weren't careful, with the excuse that they were a large family, would begin to act as if they were the only ones in the world. They even wanted to hang lines across our point to dry their washing.

But the others also had wronged the Z'zus to begin with by calling them "immigrants," on the pretext that, since the others had been there first, the Z'zus had come later. This was mere unfounded prejudice —that seems obvious to me—because neither before nor after existed, nor any place to emigrate from, but there were those who insisted that the concept of "immigrant" could be understood in the abstract, outside of space and time.

It was what you might call a narrow-minded attitude, our outlook at that time, very petty. The fault of the environment in which we had been reared. An attitude that, basically, has remained in all of us, mind you. It keeps cropping up even today if two of us happen to meet—at the bus stop, in a moviehouse, at an international dentists' convention —and start reminiscing about the old days. We say hello—at times somebody recognizes me, at other times I recognize somebody—and we promptly start asking about this one and that one (even if each remembers only a few of those remembered by the others), and so we start in again on the old disputes, the slanders, the denigrations. Until somebody mentions Mrs. $Ph(i)Nk_0$—every conversation finally gets around to her—and then, all of a sudden, the pettiness is put aside and we feel uplifted, filled with a blissful, generous emotion. Mrs. $Ph(i)Nk_0$, the only one that none of us has forgotten and that we all regret. Where has she ended up? I have long since stopped looking for her. Mrs. $Ph(i)Nk_0$, her bosom, her thighs, her orange dressing gown—we'll never meet her again, in this system of galaxies or in any other.

Let me make one thing clear: This theory that the universe, after having reached an extremity of rarefaction, will be condensed again has never convinced me. And yet many of us are counting only on that, continually making plans for the time when we'll all be back there again. Last month, I went into the bar here on the corner and whom did I see? Mr. $Pber^t Pber^d$. "What's new with you? How do you happen to be in this neighborhood?" I learned that he's the agent for a plastics firm in Pavia. He's the same as ever, with his silver tooth, his loud suspenders.

"When we go back there," he said to me in a

whisper, "the thing we have to make sure of is, this time, certain people remain out. . . . You know who I mean: those Z'zus. . . ."

I would have liked to answer him by saying that I've heard a number of people make the same remark, including, "You know who I mean: Mr. Pber^t Pber^d. . . ."

To avoid the subject, I hastened to say, "What about Mrs. Ph(i)Nk$_0$? Do you think we'll find her back there again?"

"Ah, yes. . . . She, by all means . . ." he said, turning purple.

For all of us, the hope of returning to that point means, above all, the hope of being once more with Mrs. Ph(i)Nk$_0$. (This applies even to me, though I don't believe in it.) And in that bar, as always happens, we fell to talking about her and were moved; even Mr. Pber^t Pber^d's unpleasantness faded in the face of that memory.

Mrs. Ph(i)Nk$_0$'s great secret is that she never aroused any jealousy among us. Or any gossip, either. The fact that she went to bed with her friend Mr. De XuaeauX was well known. But in a point, if there's a bed, it takes up the whole point; so it isn't a question of *going* to bed, but of *being* there, because anybody in the point is also in the bed. Consequently, it was inevitable that she should be in bed also with each of us. If she had been another person, there's no telling all the things that would have been said about her. It was the cleaning woman who always started the slander, and the others didn't have to be coaxed to imitate her. On the subject of the Z'zu family—for a change—the horrible things we had to hear; father, daughters, brothers, sisters, mother, aunts—nobody showed any hesitation, even before the most sinister insinuation. But with her, it was different. The happiness I derived from her was the joy of being concealed, punctiform, in her and of protecting her, punctiform, in me; it was at the same time vicious contemplation (thanks to the promiscuity of the punctiform convergence of us all in her) and also chastity (given her punctiform impenetrability). In short, what more could I ask?

And all of this, which was true of me, was true also for each of the others. And for her: She contained and was contained with equal happiness, and she welcomed us and loved and inhabited all equally.

We got along so well all together, so well that something extraordinary was bound to happen. It was enough for her to say at a certain moment, "Oh, if I only had some room, how I'd like to make some noodles for you boys!" And in that moment we all thought of the space that her round arms would occupy, moving backward and forward with the rolling pin over the dough, her bosom leaning over the great mound of flour and eggs that cluttered the wide board while her arms kneaded and kneaded, white and shiny with oil up to the elbows. We thought of the space that the flour would occupy, and the wheat for the flour, and the fields to raise the wheat, and the mountains from which the water would flow to irrigate the fields, and the grazing lands for the herds of calves that would give their meat for the sauce; of the space it would take for the sun to arrive with its rays to ripen the wheat; of the space for the sun to condense from the clouds of stellar gases and burn; of the quantities of stars and galaxies and galactic masses in flight through space that would be needed to hold suspended every galaxy, every nebula, every sun, every planet. And at the same time we thought of it, this space was inevitably being formed; at the same time that Mrs. Ph(i)Nk$_0$ was uttering those words—"Ah, what noodles, boys!"—the point that contained her and all of us was expanding in a halo of distance in light-years and light-centuries and billions of light-millennia, and we were being hurled to the four corners of the universe (Mr. Pbert Pberd all the way to Pavia) and she, dissolved into I don't

know what kind of energy-light-heat, she, Mrs.
Ph(i)Nk$_0$, she who in the midst of our closed, petty
world had been capable of a generous impulse—
"Boys, the noodles I would make for you!"—a true
outburst of general love, initiating at the same moment the concept of space and, properly speaking,
space itself, and time, and universal gravitation, and
the gravitating universe, making possible billions and
billions of suns, and of planets, and fields of wheat,
and Mrs. Ph(i)Nk$_0$s scattered through the continents
of the planets, kneading with floury, oil-shiny, generous arms, and her lost at that very moment, and
us mourning her loss.

GAMES WITHOUT END

*When the galaxies become more remote, the
rarefaction of the universe is compensated for by
the formation of further galaxies composed of newly
created matter. To maintain a stable median density
of the universe, it is sufficient to create a hydrogen
atom every 250 million years for 40 cubic centi-
meters of expanding space. (This steady-state theory,
as it is known, has been opposed to the other hypothesis, that the universe was born at a precise
moment as the result of a gigantic explosion.)*

I was only a child, but I was already aware of it
—*Qfwfq narrated*—I was acquainted with all the
hydrogen atoms, one by one, and when a new atom
cropped up, I noticed it right away. When I was a
kid, the only playthings we had in the whole universe were the hydrogen atoms, and we played with
them all the time, me and another youngster my age
named Pfwfp.

What sort of games? That's simple enough to explain. Since space was curved, we sent the atoms
rolling along its curve, like so many marbles, and
the kid whose atom went farthest won the game.

When you made your shot, you had to be careful, to calculate the effects, the trajectories; you had to know how to exploit the magnetic fields and the fields of gravity; otherwise, the ball left the track and was eliminated from the contest.

The rules were the usual thing: With one atom you could hit another of your atoms and send it farther ahead, or else you could knock your opponent's atom out of the way. Of course, we were careful not to throw them too hard, because when a hydrogen atom and a neutron knocked together, click!—a deuterium atom might be formed, or even a helium atom, and for the purposes of the game, such atoms were out. What's more, if one of the two belonged to your opponent, you had to give him an atom of your own to pay him back.

You know how the curve of space is shaped. A little ball would go spinning along and then one fine moment it would start off down the slope and you couldn't catch it. So, as we went on playing, the number of atoms in the game kept getting smaller, and the first to run out of atoms was the loser.

Then, right at the crucial moment, these new atoms started cropping up. Obviously, there's quite a difference between a new atom and a used one: The new atoms were shiny, bright, fresh and moist, as if with dew. We made new rules: One new was worth three old, and the new ones, as they were formed, were to be shared between us, 50-50.

In this way, our game never ended and it never became boring, either, because every time we found new atoms, it seemed as if the game were new as well, as if we were playing it for the first time.

Then, what with one thing and another, as the days went by, the game grew less exciting. There were no more new atoms to be seen. The ones we lost couldn't be replaced; our shots became weak and hesitant because we were afraid to lose the few pieces still in the game in that barren, even space.

Pfwfp was changed, too. He became absent-minded, wandered off and couldn't be found when it was his turn to shoot; I would call him, but there was never an answer, and then he would turn up half an hour later.

"Go on, it's your turn. Aren't you in the game anymore?"

"Of course I'm in the game. Don't rush me. I'm going to shoot now."

"Well, if you keep going off on your own, we might as well stop playing!"

"Hmph! You're only making all this fuss because you're losing."

This was true. I hadn't any atoms left, whereas Pfwfp, somehow or other, always had one in reserve. If some new atoms didn't turn up for us to share, I hadn't a hope of catching up with him.

The next time Pfwfp went off, I followed him on tiptoe. As long as I was present, he seemed to be strolling about aimlessly, whistling, but once he was out of my sight, he started trotting through space, intent, like somebody who has a definite purpose in mind. And what this purpose of his was—this treachery, as you shall see—I soon discovered: Pfwfp knew all the places where new atoms were formed, and every now and then he would take a walk to collect them on the spot the minute they were dished up; then he would hide them. This was why he was never short of atoms to play with!

But before putting them in the game, incorrigible cheat that he was, he set about disguising them as old atoms, rubbing the film of the electrons until it was worn and dull to make me believe this was an old atom he had had all along and had just happened to find in his pocket.

And that wasn't the whole story. I made a quick calculation of the atoms played and I realized they were only a small part of those he had stolen and hid. Was he piling up a store of hydrogen? What would he do with it? What did he have in mind? I suddenly had a suspicion: Pfwfp wanted to build a universe of his own, a brand-new universe.

From that moment on, I couldn't rest easy; I had to get even with him. I could have followed his example. Now that I knew the places, I could have gone there a little ahead of him and grabbed the new atoms the moment they were born, before he could get his hands on them! But that would have been too simple. I wanted to catch him in a trap worthy of his own perfidy. First of all, I started making fake atoms. While he was occupied with his treacherous raids, I was in a secret storeroom of mine, pounding and mixing and kneading all the material I had at my disposal. To tell you the truth, this material didn't amount to much—photoelectric radiations, scrapings from magnetic fields, a few neutrons collected in the road—but by rolling it into balls and wetting it with saliva, I managed to make it stick together. In other words, I prepared some little corpuscles that, on close inspection, were obviously not made of hydrogen or any other identifiable element, but for somebody in a hurry, like Pfwfp, who rushed past and stuck them furtively into his pocket, they looked like real hydrogen and spanking-new.

So, while he still didn't suspect a thing, I preceded him in his rounds. I had made a mental note of all the places.

Space is curved everywhere, but in some places it's more curved than in others, like pockets or bottlenecks or niches, where the void is crumpled up. These niches are where, every 250 million years, there is a slight tinkling sound and a shiny hydrogen atom is formed like a pearl between the valves of an oyster. I walked past, pocketed the atom and set the fake atom in its place. Pfwfp didn't notice a thing. Predatory, greedy, he filled his pockets with that rubbish, as I was accumulating all the treasures that the universe cherished in its bosom.

The fortunes of our games underwent a change: I always had new atoms to shoot, while Pfwfp's regularly missed fire. Three times he tried a roll and three times the atom crumbled to bits as if crushed in space. Now Pfwfp found one excuse after another, trying to call off the game.

"Go on," I insisted, "if you don't shoot, the game's mine."

And he said, "It doesn't count. When an atom is ruined, the game's null and void and you start over again." This was a rule he had invented at that very moment.

I didn't give him any peace; I danced around him, leaped on his back and chanted:

> *"Throw it throw it throw it,*
> *If not, you lose, you know it.*
> *For every turn that you don't take*
> *An extra throw for me to make."*

"That's enough of that," Pfwfp said. "Let's change games."

"Aha!" I said. "Why don't we play at flying galaxies?"

"Galaxies?" Pfwfp suddenly brightened with pleasure. "Suits me. But you . . . you don't have a galaxy!"

"Yes, I do."

"So do I."

"Come on! Let's see who can send his highest!"

And I took all the new atoms I was hiding and flung them into space. At first they seemed to scatter; then they thickened together into a kind of light cloud, and the cloud swelled and swelled, and inside it some incandescent condensations were formed, and they whirled and whirled and at a certain point became a spiral of constellations never seen before, a spiral that poised, opening in a gust, then sped away as I held on to its tail and ran after it. But now I wasn't the one who made the galaxy fly; it was the galaxy that was lifting me aloft, clinging to its tail. I mean, there wasn't any height or depth now, but only space, widening, and the galaxy in its midst also opening wide and me hanging there, making faces at Pfwfp, who was already thousands of light-years away.

Pfwfp, at my first move, had promptly dug out all his hoard, hurling it with a balanced movement, as if he expected to see the coils of an endless galaxy open in the sky. But, instead, nothing happened. There was a sizzling sound of radiations, a messy flash; then everything died out.

"Is that the best you can do?" I shouted at Pfwfp, who was yelling curses at me, green with rage.

"I'll show you, Qfwfq, you pig!"

But in the meantime, my galaxy and I were flying among thousands of other galaxies and mine was the newest, the envy of the whole firmament, blazing as it was with young hydrogen and the youngest beryllium and newborn carbon. The old galaxies fled us, filled with jealousy, and we, prancing and haughty, avoided them, so antiquated and ponderous to look at. As that reciprocal flight developed, we sailed across spaces that became more and more rarefied and empty, and then I saw something appear in the midst of the void, like uncertain bursts of light. These were new galaxies, formed by matter just born, galaxies even newer than mine. Soon space became filled again and dense, like a vineyard just before vintage time, and we flew on, escaping from one another, my galaxy fleeing the younger ones as it had the older, and young and old fleeing us. And we advanced to fly through empty skies and these skies also became peopled, and so on and on.

In one of these propagations, I heard, "Qfwfq, you'll pay for this now, you traitor!" and I saw a brand-new galaxy flying on our trail, and there, leaning forward from the very tip of the spiral,

yelling threats and insults at me, was my old play-
mate Pfwfp.

The chase began. Where space rose, Pfwfp's
galaxy, young and agile, gained ground, but on the
descents, my heavier galaxy plunged ahead again.

In any kind of race, there's a secret: It's all in
how you take the curves. Pfwfp's galaxy tended to
narrow them, mine, to swing out. And as it kept
broadening the curves, we were finally flung beyond
the edge of space, with Pfwfp after us. We kept up
the pursuit, using the system one always uses in
such circumstances, that is, creating space before
us as we went forward.

So there I was, with nothingness in front of me
and that nasty-faced Pfwfp after me—an unpleasant
sight either way. In any case, I preferred to look
ahead, and what did I see? Pfwfp, whom my eyes
had just left behind me, was speeding on his galaxy
directly in front of me. "Ah!" I cried. "Now it's my
turn to chase you!"

"What?" Pfwfp said from before me or behind
me; I'm not really sure which. "I'm the one who's
chasing you!"

I turned around. There was Pfwfp, still at my
heels. I looked ahead again. And he was there,
racing off with his back turned to me. But as I
looked more closely, I saw that in front of this
galaxy of his that was preceding me, there was
another, and that other galaxy was mine, because
there I was on it, unmistakable even though seen
from behind. And I turned toward the Pfwfp following me and narrowed my eyes. I saw that his
galaxy was being chased by another, mine, with
me on top of it, turning at that same time to look
back.

And so after every Qfwfq there was a Pfwfp,
and after every Pfwfp, a Qfwfq, and every Pfwfp was
chasing a Qfwfq, who was pursuing him, and vice
versa. Our distances grew a bit shorter or a bit

longer, but now it was clear that one would never overtake the other nor the other overtake one. We had lost all pleasure in this game of chase and we weren't children anymore, for that matter, but now there was nothing else we could do.

On Location

thomas baum

Last night I fall asleep while reading over the
script, and when I wake up this morning, I am
lying on my white leather couch in my living room
(I have a brownstone in the East 30s) and the
clock reads ten o'clock. This means I am already
late on the set, since the call is for 10:15. By now,
all the streets from my house to the Central Park
boat pond will be clogged with film crews and it will
take about an hour by car. By rights I should walk,
but I feel like a ride this morning. I call the agency
and there's a limousine waiting outside my brownstone by the time I'm dressed and ready. I'm wearing
the suit I wear in the commercial. A fine spring
day. I tell the driver Central Park and we set off.
As expected, it takes about an hour cross-town, but
I use the time to go over the script once more and
then just sit back and enjoy the view. On every cross
street there are cameras, crowds and cable, falling
past like pencils rolling off a table. Arc lamps blaze
holes in the sunlight. On Fifth Avenue, we turn
(they have made Fifth Avenue one-way uptown
again) and the big productions swing into view. In
Rockefeller Plaza, they are shooting a whimsical
savings-and-loan commercial; people are throwing

money into the fountain, and every few seconds, a
teller surfaces and makes change. The crowd seems
to be loving it. Across from St. Patrick's, they are
holding man-in-the-street interviews, and volunteers
are lined up on 50th all the way to Madison Avenue.
Zenith is videotaping a spot in its own showroom
at 53rd and Fifth: Here the crowd is being asked
to watch itself on the TVs in the window. In front of
the G.M. building, I notice a group from GS&C, the
agency that gave me my first acting job. They are
shooting a crowd scene, too, and I see one of the
producers handing out delicatessen numbers. A camera car rides our tail for two blocks, getting some
limousine footage, then swerves around us, the
cameraman saluting. Now we are at Central Park
and I notice Revlon has booked the zoo. There is a
huge crowd here, as well, and throughout the park.
The cops are on hand to ensure order, but the people
seem as cooperative and contented as ever, the more
so in retrospect, inasmuch as the grumblers—that
envious minority that circulates through all location
crowds, complaining about the traffic, the noise, the
lights, the humming of the cameras and the expro-
priation of public property—must at this moment
be massing secretly in some location of their own.

I think how it must have looked from the air, the
swarms of malcontents marching on the boat pond,
like ants converging on a drop of syrup. (Our location is among the first to be attacked.) When I
get there, around noon, everything is still proceeding
normally. The Groom & Clean reps have just arrived;
so my lateness goes unnoticed. Edie is there, already
in her mermaid costume and waiting to be trans-
ported to her rock. They are going to shoot her
alone first, and then, as the script has it, I row over
in a rowboat and we have a little conversation about
the product. The problem just now is with Edie's
rock, which the Groom & Clean reps are worried
doesn't give off enough reflection; so the crew is

hosing it with glycerin. Edie, squirming around in her mermaid costume, looks about to throw a sulk. When I go over, though, I see she is not so much impatient or sulky as, for some reason, scared.

"Well, let them get the thing right and we can all go home," I say.

"Something weird going on," she says.

"Like what?"

"I just don't want to be here. I don't know what it is."

"Is it the costume? It's a nice costume."

"I just have this weird feeling."

That's all the warning we have. We wait as everything is moved up, the cameras, the lights, the reflectors, and the crowd gathers at the shore line, out of range, eating their lunch out of paper bags. The make-up people come and put the stuff in my hair, with the FTC guy hovering to make sure it's the real thing, right out of the tube. I'm not in the first shot; so I wander off up a nearby slope to watch. Some people in the crowd start to follow me, thinking the next setup will be on the hill, where I'm going, but I assure them no, pointing to the rowboats, and they go back to watch Edie. So I'm alone, looking down on the boat pond, with a view of other locations in the park—Salem and Clairol and Pepsi—and I'm the first to spot the attackers. I don't even know what to call them. The enemy? Long lines strung back toward Fifth. What the crew on the ground sees is a few noisy latecoming spectators, maybe a few grumblers, but from the slope where I am, it's the organized aspect that is obvious, and then I see the weapons. I can't believe it. Guns. Not all of the attackers have guns, but a lot of them do and they are converging on Salem and Clairol and Pepsi and on all of us at the pond. Little by little, it is dawning on the people below. I manage to signal to one of the cops, who starts over with some men. Then, in the distance, I hear one of the attackers, one of the enemy leaders, cry out, "Are the cops the only ones preventing you from entering this location?" "No!" the yell comes back, enthusiastic, obedient, followed by a confused pause, and then the voice of the leader trying again: "Aren't they? Listen, now. I say, aren't the cops the only ones keeping you from this location?" "Yes!" comes the answer, the correct one this time, and cries of "Death to the expropriators!" "Death to the image makers!" "Death to the manipulators!" Our people, the crew, the Groom & Clean reps, are running for cover, while the first attackers to reach the location are timidly overturning canvas chairs, still not sure of the procedure and looking around at the leaders for instructions. But nobody is stopping them; the cops, who have never seen such a thing, are slow to respond and the attack is gathering momentum. One of the propmen is blowing a whistle. I try to make an inconspicuous descent from the slope. As I climb down, baboon fashion, something lands with a splash in the pond; they are starting to throw things in, a light stand, a coil of wire. There is a crackle of bad electricity and the pond gives off a puff of smoke. This is real trouble. Our people are milling around in confusion. The invaders have begun to intimidate the bystanders, thrusting guns into their hands and commanding them to join the assault. Another splash. I look behind me and see a camera crane being wheeled to the side of the pond and tipped in, and then comes the unmistakable sound of human bodies being thrown into the waters. I look around for Edie and then I see her. Two of the leaders are trying to carry her off, as though she were a trophy, but she is flailing around in her mermaid costume and the two men are finding her a slippery catch. I run toward her. The costume has come unzipped; one breast is exposed. I lunge at one of the leaders. He drops Edie and wheels around, getting tangled in his gunstrap. His eyes light up and I see I am a

trophy, too. I grab the other leader around the neck
and he lets go of Edie, who is free now, running
across the grass to where my limousine is parked; in
the next moment, I pull loose from the second attacker, hearing a shot go off above my head, and
soon I am in the car, our location a shambles behind
us. We are heading back toward Fifth, my whole
body tingling. Edie is shaking. When I get hold of
myself, I flip on the TV. A news helicopter is swooping low over midtown; it is clear the trouble has
spread to nearly every location. But Edie and I can
see this for ourselves, out the window. As we turn
onto Fifth, a crowd surges out of the zoo with a
Revlon model borne aloft on several pairs of hands.
Ahead, on 66th Street, a Chef Boy-ar-dee Pizza car is
aflame, with an actor inside. Edie, her nipple flat-
tened against the windowpane, cries out in horror.

"Call somebody," she says, clutching my sleeve.
"Are they going to let these people just do this?
Where are all the police?"

"Caught napping, I guess." I try the car phone.
One line is dead. I hang up and try again. This time
I get an open line, but an actress imitating an oper-
ator repeats the words *directory assistance* three
times; I hear a voice in the background say, "Cut."

"They're pretty smart," I say. "Some of the locations they're leaving alone. Letting us strangle in
our own cable, as it were."

"How can you be so smug about it?"

"Am I?"

"It's all your fault," she says.

"Why my fault?"

"You should have seen it coming," she says,
tugging at her mermaid costume.

"So we could have joined the right side?"

"Yes. All right. Why, did you *like* being an actor
so much?"

"You're speaking in the past tense."

"With your hair full of grease. And me in this

idiot costume." She shakes her head, biting back an inadvertent smile. We are nearing my house in the East 30s now, the driver steering a course through unruly crowds. "I can't believe it. And we're sitting here arguing—almost joking—about it."

"I guess this is the time we do joke," I reply. The truth is, I am sexually aroused. There is a sound of gunfire in the distance. My head is snapping with it. I suppose I still don't believe it's happening, though as we get out of the car in front of my house, recalling that Edie and I are special targets, I am careful to look both ways before heading up the stairs. At the head of my street, a camera car has been forced to the curb by a group of attackers. Shielding Edie, I open the front door. We go inside. I lock the door. I go down to the basement and check the courtyard door. I pull down all the blinds and return to the living room, where Edie is seated on my leather couch, trying to undo her zipper. My living room looks suddenly so incriminating: the pictures of myself on the walls, stills from various commercials and my two Clios from the American TV and Radio Commercials Festival on the mantelpiece. I recoil in fastidious horror, as though I had wandered by mistake into a Ripley's Believe It or Not museum. It is not my house. I never meant to live like this. Should I hide my picture? Or will the cops have things under control in a few hours? The clock on my coffee table reads 1:30. Maybe all we have to do is hold out; by tomorrow everything will be normal again—better than normal, because now the enemy has exposed itself and can be exterminated. I am very excited. I go over to help Edie, who is still cursing at her mermaid zipper, and thrust my hand between the couch and her scaly, sequined leg. As soon as I touch her costume, I feel everything is going to be all right. I peel it down and pry into her popliteal fossa, firm pad defined by photogenic tendons, the supple, moist flesh, while Edie sits there smiling, excited, as bewildered as I am that we can be making love in the midst of possible disaster, yet letting me know with a smile that she, too, has decided this is what people everywhere have always done. Her head goes back, her body slips gently down, her nostrils widen as I bare her hips to the light and kiss her mouth, tasting a thick, molten bubble, like the center of a clay spring, which breaks, spreading its flavor over my lips.

She starts to murmur, then twists her head in alarm. A second light has just gone on in my living room. A footstep hooks us like two fish. Jerking up, we see a figure in the doorway.

It is the man from the boat pond. One of the two leaders who tried to carry Edie off. He has followed us here. He is fiercely calm and is pointing his gun at us. Here. In my living room. But if a man is in your house, how can he be your enemy? And now, with a sweep of the gun barrel, he knocks all the items off my mantelpiece, including my two Clios. My face goes hot. I am going to cry. Edie is clutching my arm. I try to open my mouth to say something, but I can't find the words and my jaw starts to tremble. "You stupid bastard," he says, raising the gun to shoot. I push Edie to one side and duck. The gun goes off. Something enters my shoulder. I dive at the attacker. The gun goes off again, into the ceiling. The man is on his back. I step on his face and wrench the gun from his hands, slamming the butt against the side of his head. I hit him again, again, digging at his skull with a hoelike motion until my arms go weak and I can hardly see through my tears. It feels as though I have been hitting him for hours. I look at his head—he is bleeding freely from the ear—and sickness engulfs me. Edie is shouting my name. A numbness crawls up my arm, burrows inside my shirt like a small animal. I feel my shoulder, wincing at a pain no larger than a tooth, wondering if there is a bullet there beneath the blood

and what must be done about that and how soon.
My lung has been punctured, I think, and test this
hypothesis with the next few breaths. The childish
fears are much worse than the pain, worse even than
the sight of a murdered man lying on my living-
room floor. I must get myself to a hospital. I go to
the door. Edie takes a raincoat from my closet to
cover herself and follows. In the midst of everything,
the sensation is like emerging from a double feature
to find the weather has changed. The East Side is
now swarming with attackers. We walk toward the
river. A captured camera car is going along First
Avenue and two men, knee deep in photographic
equipment, are tossing cameras and lenses and film
stock onto the sidewalk, cheered on by a crowd
standing in front of Bellevue. We cross the street.
Fires have broken out all along First Avenue. All
the locations have been sacked except the vital
services. They are treating their own wounded at
the hospital. "Our own wounded," I say aloud. Edie
winces. My wound is starting to throb. In the Bellevue parking lot, guns are being distributed. We walk
toward the entrance. Medics are watching from the
doorway. I go over, clutching the gun. A medic
peels off my shirt. "Death to the image makers," I
say. The medic nods. There are many people
tightly packed in the parking lot, camera cars and
ambulances coming and going, men with rifles climbing onto trucks, dismounting, new shifts of attackers
being dispatched in camera cars to new locations.
I look around for Edie, lost somewhere in the crowd.
The medic is bandaging my shoulder. "You're
needed," he says, acknowledging the gun I hold and
pointing to a car about to leave for somewhere.

"The girl I was with——"

"Has been sent to Central Park."

I suppress a shudder. "To mop up?"

"Exactly."

Oh, God, I think, but they have won and I am in

the car, pulling away from the hospital onto First Avenue. The streets are filled with broken glass. Across First, at the Kips Bay apartments, gunfire is coming from the roof. I want to roll down the window, call out, tell everyone to give up. We should have known. To tie up public property is evil. A camera car is going by. They must have salvaged some equipment, because they have a camera pointed at us and running. The barbarians donning Roman finery, I think, feeling the car slow up. It is my house we are stopping at. Oh, God. They don't realize a man has already come here. They will find him on my living-room floor with his skull crushed in. They'll see my picture on the wall. Oh, God.

I wonder if I can make a run for it. I have left my rifle in the car and now they are forcing me up the stairs into my own house. I shake myself free and rush into my living room.

There is no one lying on my floor. I look up and see the dead man giving me a wink. A make-up man is wiping his temple clean of blood. I turn around and see the cameras and lights being moved in and a propman replacing my Clios on the mantelpiece. Another propman is setting back the clock on my coffee table. He leaves it at ten o'clock, then unwinds the bloody bandage from my shoulder and discards it. A third propman places a script face down next to the clock. Turning, I can see the director seated in a canvas chair, the cameraman stepping behind his camera and, behind them, a crowd of onlookers being kept at a distance by several policemen. I am told to lie back on my white leather couch and pretend to be waking up. I close my eyes and lights come on and a camera hums as the horror of it strikes me: They are going to do this until they get it right.

Man with a Past

t. k. brown III

"For the person asleep," Professor Pickering said, "time, in a sense, stands still. When he regains consciousness, he has jumped a certain interval into the future. Indeed, there have been cases of prolonged coma lasting many years, from which the patient has awakened to an entirely alien world."

"It would appear to be somewhat more difficult to leap into the past," Professor Dickson remarked dryly.

"Yet I have done it!" Professor Pickering said, his eyes flashing through his bifocals and his white goatee jutting forward. "I have done it and have come back! To state it simply, it was a matter of detecting the principles involved and building the instrument to apply them. The recent advances in electroencephalography were an immense help; I was fortunate enough to discover that the electrical impulses of brain action could be harnessed to the practical needs of time exploration."

Dickson could not keep the note of incredulity from his voice. "You are not trying to tell me, old friend, that you have visited the past with the help of some contrivance."

By way of answer, Professor Pickering went to the

bookcase and took down a volume. "I was present at Lincoln's Gettysburg Address," he said with dignity. "I appear in this book of Mathew Brady's Civil War photographs." He flipped open to the page in question and pointed to a figure in the audience. "It would be hard to mistake me," he said. "Please make use of this magnifying glass."

Professor Dickson laughed heartily. "Good Lord, man, I trust you will not be so ill advised as to offer this to anyone but a close friend as evidence of anything whatsoever. Why, everyone in this picture looks like everyone else."

Professor Pickering took from his pocket a box about the size of a matchbox (large kitchen-size). "With this dial," he said, "I register the number of years I wish to regress; with this one I select the longitude and latitude of my destination. I have long wished to visit Elizabethan England and have already ascertained the precise location of Sir Francis Bacon's estate in Gorhamburg, where he was in residence in 1622. I believe I will drop in on Sir Francis."

"No doubt he will find your accent rather bizarre," Professor Dickson said, "to say nothing of your dress."

"Yes, clothing is a problem, since I intend to visit several widely different cultures. I am wearing these slacks and this T-shirt in the hope that they will attract a minimum of attention. In any event, I am prepared to make a hasty departure from whatever times and places I visit." So saying, he made a final adjustment on his dials and pressed a button on the side of the box. Professor Dickson was dumfounded to see his friend disappear before his eyes—at the same instant that Sir Francis Bacon, taking the air in his garden, was no less surprised to see a stranger materialize in the rose bed.

"How now, varlet?" said Sir Francis.

"I'll only trouble you for a minute," Pickering

said. "Just tell me one thing. Are you the author of the plays attributed to William Shakespeare?"

"Of course not," Sir Francis said testily. "What ever gave you that crazy idea? They were all written by Eddie de Vere, seventeenth Earl of Oxford."

"Thank you," said the professor. "Several of my colleagues will be pained to hear it." And with that he adjusted his little box, pushed the button and showed up on the steps of the Roman Senate on March 15, 44 B.C., just in time to witness the stabbing of Julius Caesar. It took place very much as Eddie de Vere had set it down.

Thereafter, he ricocheted around in ancient history; it is hardly necessary to detail his adventures. It was while he was watching the building of the Great Pyramid at Giza that he resolved to take the big plunge. *How did things begin?* The origins of man? The beginnings of life itself? He could always come back to these relatively modern times.

For his first stopover, he set the machine to take him back 500,000 years and to set him in the African Transvaal, where the most recent findings of paleoanthropology had placed the earliest traces of man's direct ancestors.

Professor Pickering pressed the button.

And that, for all practical purposes, was the end of Professor Pickering.

Did he tumble off a cliff? Fall prey to some prehistoric monster? Get his head knocked in by his xenophobic fellow man? No, he arrived safely and met with no physical mishap.

What he had not known, however, was that, as he moved further and further into the past, he was actually retracing the line of his forebears, backward through the generations, backward through the evolution of the race. So long as he had confined himself to historical times, his retreat down the evolutionary ladder was too slight to matter and his personality, state of knowledge and memory remained intact, but when he took the half-million-year leap——

Professor Pickering (emeritus now) scampered nimbly up the baobab tree, the only white-goateed Australopithecine ape in all Africa with bifocals, slacks and T-shirt—and a brain much too stupid to know what to do with that funny little box in his pocket.

Word of Honor

robert bloch

At 2:27 in the afternoon, Homer Gans, cashier, entered the office of his employer, the president of the First National Bank.

"I've got something to tell you," he murmured. "It's about the reserve fund. I'm into it for forty thousand dollars."

"You're *what?*"

"I embezzled from the reserve fund," Homer said. "Been doing it for years now, and nobody ever caught on. Some of the money went to play the races, and a lot of it has been paying somebody's rent. You wouldn't think to look at me that I'd be keeping a blonde on the side. But then, you don't know how it is at home."

The president frowned. "Oh, yes, I do," he answered, taking a deep breath. "As a matter of fact, I happen to be keeping a blonde myself. Though to tell the truth, she isn't a natural blonde."

Homer hesitated, then sighed. "To tell the truth," he said, "neither is mine."

Between 2:28 and 2:43, quite a number of things happened. A model nephew told his rich and elderly uncle to go to hell and quit trying to run his life. An equally model husband told his wife he had hated her and their children for years and frequently wished they'd all drop dead. A star shoe salesman told a female customer to quit wasting time trying on small sizes and go out and buy a couple of rowboats. At one of the embassies, a visiting diplomat paused in the midst of a flattering toast and abruptly emptied the contents of his glass upon the bald head of the American ambassador.

And——

"Holy Toledo!" howled Wally Tibbets, managing editor of the *Daily Express*. "Has everybody flipped?"

Reporter Joe Satterlee shrugged.

"In nine years on this rag, I've never pulled that 'Stop the presses!' stuff. But we're standing by for a replate right now—and we're going to stand by until we find out what gives. Got enough lead copy for a dozen front pages right now, and none of it makes sense."

"Such as?" Satterlee gazed calmly at his boss.

"Take your pick. Our senior senator just issued a statement of resignation—says he's unfit to hold office. That labor leader who built the big new union headquarters uptown went and shot himself. Police headquarters can't keep up with the guys who are coming in and confessing everything from murder to mopery. And if you think that's something, you ought to hear what's going on down in the advertising department. Clients are canceling space like mad. Three of the biggest used-car dealers in town just yanked their ads."

Joe Satterlee yawned. "What goes on here?"

"That's just what I want you to find out. And fast." Wally Tibbets stood up. "Go see somebody and get a statement. Try the university. Tackle the science department."

Satterlee nodded and went downstairs to his car.

Traffic seemed to be disrupted all over the city, and something had happened to the pedestrians. Some of them were running and the others moved along in a daze or merely stood silently in the center of the sidewalk. Faces had lost their usual mask of immobility. Some people laughed and others wept. Over in the grass of the university campus, a number of couples lay locked in close embrace, oblivious of still other couples who were fighting furiously. Joe Satterlee blinked at what he saw and drove on.

At 3:02 he drove up to the administration building. A burly man stood on the curb, doing a little dance of impatience. He looked as though he wanted either a taxi or a washroom, but fast.

"Pardon me," Satterlee said. "Is Dean Hanson's office in this building?"

"I'm Hanson," the burly man snapped.

"My name's Satterlee. I'm with the *Daily Express*——"

"Good Lord, do they know already?"

"Know what?"

"Never mind." Dean Hanson shook his head. "Can't talk to you now. Got to find a cab. I suppose I'll never get to the airport."

"Leaving town?"

"No. I've got to get my hands on Dr. Lowenquist. He's at the bottom of all this——"

Satterlee opened the door. "Come on, get in," he said. "I'll drive you to the airport. We can talk on the way."

A wind came out of the west and the sun disappeared to cower behind a cloud.

"Storm coming up," Dean Hanson muttered. "That damned fool better land before it hits."

"Lowenquist," Satterlee said. "Isn't he head of the school of dentistry?"

"That's right," Hanson sighed. "All this nonsense about mad scientists is bad enough, but a mad *dentist*——"

"What did he do?"

"He chartered a plane this afternoon, all by himself, and took it up over the city. He's been spraying the town with that gas of his," Hanson sighed. "I don't know anything about science. I'm just a poor university dean, and my job is to get money out of rich alumni. But the way I hear it, Lowenquist was monkeying around with chemical anesthetics. He mixed up a new combination—like Pentothal sodium, sodium Amytal—only a lot stronger and more concentrated."

"Aren't those used in psychotherapy, for narcohypnosis?" Satterlee asked. "What they call truth serums?"

"This isn't a serum. It's a gas."

"You can say that again," Satterlee agreed. "So he waited for a clear, windless day and went up in a plane to dust the city with a concentrated truth gas. Is that a fact?"

"Of course it is," Hanson replied. "You know I can't lie to you." He sighed again. "Nobody can lie anymore. Apparently the stuff is so powerful that one sniff does the trick. Psychiatry department gives me a lot of flap about inhibitory release and bypassing the superego and if a man answers, hang up. But what it all boils down to is the gas *works*. Everybody who was outside, everybody with an open window or an air-conditioning unit was affected. Almost the entire city. They can't lie anymore. They don't even *want* to lie."

"Wonderful!" Satterlee exclaimed, glancing up at the gathering storm clouds.

"Is it? I'm not so sure. When the story hits the papers, it'll give the whole school a bad name. I shouldn't even have told you, but I can't help myself. I just feel the need to be frank about everything. That's what I was telling my secretary, before she slapped my face——"

Satterlee wheeled into the airport. "That your

boy up there?" He pointed upward at a small plane careening between the clouds in the sudden gale.

"Yes," Hanson shouted. "He's trying to come in for a landing, I think. But the wind's too strong——"

A sudden lance of lightning pierced the sky. The plane wobbled and began to spin.

Satterlee gunned the motor and turned off onto the field. In the distance a siren wailed and, through the rushing rain, he could see the plane spiraling down in a crazy dive. . . .

• • •

Wally Tibbets leaned back and pushed his chair away from the desk.

"That's how it happened," Satterlee told him. "The poor guy was dead before they pulled him out of the wreckage. But they found the tanks and equipment. He had the papers on him, and I persuaded Hanson to turn the stuff over to me; he was in such a daze, he didn't even think to object. So now we can back up the story with proof. I've got copies of the formula he discovered. I suppose we'll feed the dope in to the wire services, too."

Tibbets shook his head. "Nope, I'm going to answer all inquiries with a flat denial."

"But the story——"

"Isn't going to be any story. All over now, anyway. Didn't you notice how people changed after that storm hit! Wind must have blown the gas away. Everyone's back to normal. Most of them have already convinced themselves that nothing ever happened."

"But we *know* it did! What about all those story leads you got this afternoon?"

"Killed. Ever since the storm, we've been getting denials and retractions. Turns out the senator isn't resigning after all—he's running for governor. The labor boy's shooting himself was an accident. The police can't get anyone to sign their confessions. The advertisers are placing new copy again. Mark my words, by tomorrow morning this whole town will have forgotten—they'll *will* themselves to forget. Nobody can face the truth and remain sane."

"That's a terrible way to think," Satterlee said. "Dr. Lowenquist was a great man. He knew his discovery could work—not just here but everywhere. After this trial run, he meant to take a plane up over Washington, fly over Moscow, all the capitals of the world. Because this truth gas could *change* the world. Don't you see that?"

"Of course I see it. But the world shouldn't be changed."

"Why not?" Satterlee squared his shoulders. "Look here, I've been thinking. I have the formula. I could carry on where Lowenquist left off. I've saved some money. I could hire pilots and planes. Don't you think the world needs a dose of truth?"

"No. You saw what happened here today on just a small scale."

"Yes. Criminals confessed, crooks reformed, people stopped lying to one another. Is that so bad?"

"About the criminals, no. But for ordinary human beings, this could be a terrible thing. You don't see what happens when the doctor tells his patient that he's dying of cancer, when the wife tells her husband he's not actually the father of their son. Everybody has secrets, or almost everybody. It's better not to know the whole truth—about others or about yourself."

"But look at what goes on in the world today."

"I am looking. That's my job—to sit at this desk and watch the world go round. Sometimes it's a dizzy spin, but at least it keeps going. Because people keep going. And they need lies to help them. Lies about abstract justice and romantic love everlasting. The belief that right always triumphs. Even our concept of democracy may be a lie. Yet we cherish these lies and do our best to live by them. And maybe, little by little, our belief helps make these things come true. It's a slow process, but in the long run it seems to work. Animals don't lie, you know. Only human beings know how to pretend, how to make believe, how to deceive themselves and others. But that's why they're human beings."

"Maybe so," Satterlee said. "Yet think of the opportunity I have. I could even stop war."

"Perhaps. Military and political leaders might face up to the truth about their motives and change —temporarily."

"We could keep on spraying," Satterlee broke in eagerly. "There are other honest men. We'd raise funds, make this a long-term project. And who knows? Perhaps after a few doses, the change would become permanent. Don't you understand? We could end war!"

"I understand," Tibbets told him. "You could end war between nations. And start hundreds of millions of *individual* wars instead. Wars waged in human minds and human hearts. There'd be a wave of insanity, a wave of suicides, a wave of murders. There'd be a tidal inundation of truth that would drown the home, the family, the whole social structure."

"I realize it's a risk. But think of what we all might gain."

Tibbets put his hand on the younger man's shoulder. "I want you to forget this whole business," he said soberly. "Don't plan to manufacture this gas and spray it over the Capitol or the Kremlin. Don't do it, for all our sakes."

Satterlee was silent, staring out into the night. Far in the distance, a jet plane screamed.

"You're an honest man," Tibbets said. "One of

the few. I dig that, and I admire you for it. But you've got to be realistic and see things my way. All I want is for you to tell me now that you won't try anything foolish. Leave the world the way it is." He paused. "Will you give me your word of honor?"

Satterlee hesitated. He *was* an honest man, he realized, and so his answer was a long time coming. Then, "I promise," Satterlee lied.

The Lost City of Mars

ray bradbury

The great eye floated in space. And behind the great eye somewhere, hidden away within metal and machinery, was a small eye that belonged to a man who looked and could not stop looking at all the multitudes of stars and the diminishings and growings of light a billion billion miles away.

The small eye closed with tiredness. Captain John Wilder stood holding to the telescopic devices that probed the universe and at last murmured, "Which one?"

The astronomer with him said, "Take your pick."

"I wish it were that easy." Wilder opened his eyes. "What's the data on that last star?"

"Same size and reading as our sun. Planetary system possible."

"Possible. Not certain. If we pick the wrong star, God help the people we send on a two-hundred year journey to find a planet that may not be there. No, God help me, for the final selection is mine, and I may well send myself on that journey. So how can we be sure?"

"We can't. We just make the best guess, send our starship out and pray."

"You are not very encouraging. That's it. I'm tired."

Wilder touched a switch that shut up tight the greater eye, this rocket-powered space lens that stared cold upon the abyss, saw far too much and knew little, and now knew nothing. The rocket laboratory drifted sightless on an endless night.

"Home," said the captain. "Let's go home."

And the blind beggar-after-stars wheeled on a spread of fire and ran away.

● ● ●

The frontier cities on Mars looked very fine from above. Coming down for a landing, Wilder saw the neons among the blue hills and thought, We'll light some worlds a billion miles off, and the children of the people living under these lights this instant, we'll make them immortal. Very simply, if we succeed, they will live forever.

Live forever. The rocket landed. Live forever.

The wind that blew from the frontier town smelled of grease. An aluminum-toothed jukebox banged somewhere. A junk yard rusted beside the rocketport. Old newspapers danced alone on the windy tarmac.

Wilder, motionless at the top of the gantry elevator, suddenly wished not to move down. The lights suddenly had become people and not words that, huge in the mind, could be handled with elaborate ease.

He sighed. The freight of people was too heavy. The stars were too far away.

"Captain?" said someone behind him.

He stepped forward. The elevator gave way. They sank with a silent screaming toward a very real land with real people in it, who were waiting for him to choose.

At midnight the telegram bin hissed and exploded out a message projectile. Wilder, at his desk, surrounded by tapes and computation cards, did not touch it for a long while. When at last he pulled the message out, he scanned it, rolled it in a tight ball, then uncrumpled the message and read again:

FINAL CANAL BEING FILLED TOMORROW WEEK. YOU ARE INVITED CANAL YACHT PARTY. DISTINGUISHED GUESTS. FOUR-DAY JOURNEY TO SEARCH FOR LOST CITY. KINDLY ACKNOWLEDGE.

I. V. AARONSON.

Wilder blinked and laughed quietly. He crumpled the paper again, but stopped, lifted the telephone and said:

"Telegram to I. V. Aaronson, Mars City I. Answer affirmative. No sane reason why, but still—affirmative."

And hung up the phone. To sit for a long while watching this night that shadowed all the whispering, ticking and motioning machines.

• • •

The dry canal waited.

It had been waiting 20,000 years for nothing but dust to filter through in ghost tides.

Now, quite suddenly, it whispered.

And the whisper became a rush and wall-caroming glide of waters.

As if a vast machined fist had struck the rocks somewhere, clapped the air and cried, "Miracle!" a wall of water came proud and high along the channel and lay down in all the dry places of the canal and moved on toward ancient deserts of dry bone, surprising old wharves and lifting up the skeletons of boats abandoned countless centuries before when the water burned away to nothing.

The tide turned a corner and lifted up—a boat as fresh as the morning itself, with new-minted silver screws and brass pipings, and bright new

Earth-sewn flags. The boat, suspended from the side of the canal, bore the name *Aaronson I.*

Inside the boat, a man with the same name smiled. Mr. Aaronson sat listening to the waters, live under the boat.

And the sound of the water was cut across by the sound of a hovercraft, arriving, and a motor bike, arriving, and in the air, as if summoned with magical timing, drawn by the glimmer of tides in the old canal, a number of gadfly people flew over the hills on jet-pack machines and hung suspended as if doubting this collision of lives caused by one rich man.

Scowling up with a smile, the rich man called to his children, cried them in from the heat with offers of food and drink.

"Captain Wilder! Mr. Parkhill! Mr. Beaumont!"

Wilder set his hovercraft down.

Sam Parkhill discarded his motor bike, for he had seen the yacht and it was a new love.

"My God," cried Beaumont, the actor, part of the frieze of people in the sky dancing like bright bees on the wind. "I've timed my entrance wrong. I'm early. There's no audience!"

"I'll applaud you down!" shouted the old man and did so, then added, "Mr. Aikens!"

"Aikens?" said Parkhill. "The big-game hunter?"

"None other!"

And Aikens dived down as if to seize them in his harrying claws. He fancied his resemblance to the hawk. He was finished and stropped like a razor by the swift life he had lived. Not an edge of him but cut the air as he fell, a strange plummeting vengeance upon people who had done nothing to him. In the moment before destruction, he pulled up on his jets and, gently screaming, simmered himself to touch the marble jetty. About his lean middle hung a rifle belt. His pockets bulged like those of a boy from the candy store. One guessed he was stashed with sweet bullets and rare bombs. In his hands, like an evil child, he held a weapon that looked like a bolt of lightning fallen straight from the clutch of Zeus, stamped, nevertheless, MADE IN U.S.A. His face was sun-blasted dark. His eyes were cool surprises in the sun-wrinkled flesh, all mint-blue-green crystal. He wore a white porcelain smile set in African sinews. The earth did not quite tremble as he landed.

"The lion prowls the land of Judah!" cried a voice from the heavens. "Now do behold the lambs driven forth to slaughter!"

"Oh, for God's sake, Harry, shut up!" said a woman's voice.

And two more kites fluttered their souls, their dread humanity, on the wind.

The rich man jubilated.

"Harry Harpwell!"

"Behold the angel of the Lord who comes with annunciations!" the man in the sky said, hovering. "And the annunciation is——"

"He's drunk again," his wife supplied, flying ahead of him, not looking back.

"Megan Harpwell," said the rich man, like an entrepreneur introducing his troupe.

"The poet," said Wilder.

"And the poet's barracuda wife," muttered Parkhill.

"I am not drunk," the poet shouted down the wind. "I am simply *high*." And here he let loose such a deluge of laughter that those below almost raised their hands to ward off the avalanche.

Lowering himself, like a fat dragon kite, the poet, whose wife's mouth was now clamped shut, bumbled over the yacht. He made the motions of blessing same and winked at Wilder and Parkhill.

"Harpwell," he called. "Isn't that a name to go with being a great modern poet who suffers in the present, lives in the past, steals bones from old dramatists' tombs and flies on this new egg-beater wind-suck device, to call down sonnets on your head? I pity the old euphoric saints and angels who had no invisible wings like these so as to dart in oriole convolutions and ecstatic convulsions on the air as they sang their lines or damned souls to hell. Poor earth-bound sparrows, wings clipped. Only their genius flew. Only their muse knew airsickness——"

"Harry," said his wife, her feet on the ground, eyes shut.

"Hunter!" called the poet. "Aikens! Here's the greatest game in all the world, a poet on the wing. I bare my breast. Let fly your honeyed bee sting! Bring me, Icarus, down, if your gun be sunbeams kindled in one tube, let free in single forest fires that escalate the sky to turn tallow, mush, candlewick and lyre to mere tar babe. Ready, aim, fire!"

The hunter, in good humor, raised his gun.

The poet, at this, laughed a mightier laugh and, literally, exposed his chest by tearing aside his shirt.

At which moment a quietness came along the canal rim.

A woman appeared, walking. Her maid walked behind her. There was no vehicle in sight, and it seemed almost as if they had wandered a long way out of the Martian hills and now stopped.

The very quietness of her entrance gave dignity and attention to Cara Corelli.

The poet shut up his lyric in the sky and landed.

The company all looked together at this actress who gazed back without seeing them. She was dressed in a black jump suit that was the same color as her dark hair. She walked like a woman who has spoken little in her life and now stood facing them with the same quietness, as if waiting for someone to move without being ordered. The wind blew her hair out and down over her shoulders. The paleness of her face was shocking. Her paleness, rather than her eyes, stared at them.

Then, without a word, she stepped down into the yacht and sat in the front of the craft, like a figure-head that knows its place and goes there.

The moment of silence was over.

Aaronson ran his finger down the printed guest list.

"An actor, a beautiful woman who happens to be an actress, a hunter, a poet, a poet's wife, a rocket captain, a former technician. All aboard!"

On the afterdeck of the huge craft, Aaronson spread forth his maps.

"Ladies, gentlemen," he said. "This is more than a four-day drinking bout, party, excursion. This is a search!"

He waited for their faces to light properly, and for them to glance from his eyes to the charts, and then said:

"We are seeking the fabled Lost City of Mars, once called Dia-Sao, the City of Doom. Something terrible about it. The inhabitants fled as from a plague. The City left empty. Still empty now, centuries later."

"We," said Captain Wilder, "have charted, mapped and cross-indexed every acre of land on Mars in the last fifteen years. You can't mislay a city the size of the one you speak of."

"True," said Aaronson, "you've mapped it from the sky, from the land. But you have *not* charted it via water, for the canals have been empty until now! So we shall take the new waters that fill this last canal and go where the boats once went in the olden days, and see the very last new things that need to be seen on Mars." The rich man continued, "And somewhere in our traveling, as sure as the breath in our mouths, we shall find the most beautiful, the most fantastic, the most awful city in the history of this old world. And walk in that city and—who

knows?—find the reason why the Martians ran
screaming away from it, as the legend says, thousands of years ago."

Silence. Then:

"Bravo! Well done." The poet shook the old
man's hand.

"And in that city," said Aikens, the hunter,
"mightn't there be weapons the like of which we've
never seen?"

"Most likely, sir."

"Well." The hunter cradled his bolt of lightning.
"I was bored of Earth, shot every animal, ran fresh
out of beasts and came here looking for newer,
better, more dangerous man-eaters of any size or
shape. Plus, now, new weapons! What more can
one ask? Fine!"

And he dropped his blue-silver lightning bolt over
the side. It sank in the clear water, bubbling.

"Let's get the hell out of here."

"Let us, indeed," said Aaronson, "get the good
hell out."

And he pressed the button that launched the
yacht.

And the water flowed the yacht away.

And the yacht went in the direction toward which
Cara Corelli's quiet paleness was pointed: beyond.

The poet opened the first champagne bottle. The
cork banged. Only the hunter did not jump.

● ● ●

The yacht sailed steadily through the day into
night. They found an ancient ruin and had dinner
there and a good wine imported 100 million miles
from Earth. It was noted that it had traveled well.

With the wine came the poet, and after quite a
bit of the poet came sleep on board the yacht that
moved away in search of a city that would not as
yet be found.

At three in the morning, restless, unaccustomed

to the gravity of a planet pulling at all of his body and not freeing him to dream, Wilder came out on the afterdeck of the yacht and found the actress there.

She was watching the waters slip by in dark revelations and discardments of stars.

He sat beside her and thought a question.

Just as silently, Cara Corelli asked herself the same question, and answered it.

"I am here on Mars because not long ago for the first time in my life, a man told me the truth."

Perhaps she expected surprise. Wilder said nothing. The boat moved as on a stream of soundless oil.

"I am a beautiful woman. I have been beautiful all of my life. Which means that from the start people lied because they simply wished to be with me. I grew up surrounded by the untruths of men, women and children who could not risk my displeasure. When beauty pouts, the world trembles.

"Have you ever seen a beautiful woman surrounded by men, seen them nodding, nodding? Heard their laughter? Men will laugh at anything a beautiful woman says. Hate themselves, yes, but they will laugh, say no for yes and yes for no.

"Well, that's how it was every day of every year for me. A crowd of liars stood between me and anything unpleasant. Their words dressed me in silks.

"But quite suddenly, oh, no more than six weeks ago, this man told me a truth. It was a small thing. I don't remember now what it was he said. But he didn't laugh. He didn't even smile.

"And no sooner was it out and over, the words spoken, than I knew a terrible thing had happened.

"I was growing old."

The yacht rocked gently on the tide.

"Oh, there would be more men who would, lying, smile again at what I said. But I saw the years ahead, when beauty could no longer stomp its small foot and shake down earthquakes, make cowardice a custom among otherwise good men.

"The man? He took back his truth immediately when he saw that he had shocked me. But it was too late. I bought a one-way fare to Mars. Aaronson's invitation, when I arrived, put me on this new journey that will end . . . who knows where."

Wilder found that during this last he had reached out and taken her hand.

"No," she said, withdrawing. "No word. No touch. No pity. No self-pity." She smiled for the first time. "Isn't it strange? I always thought, Wouldn't it be nice, someday, to hear the truth, to give up the masquerade? How wrong I was. It's no fun at all."

She sat and watched the black waters pour by the boat. When she thought to look again, some hours later, the seat beside her was empty. Wilder was gone.

● ● ●

On the second day, letting the new waters take them where it wished to go, they sailed toward a high range of mountains and lunched on the way in an old shrine and had dinner that night in a further ruin. The Lost City was not much talked about. They were sure it would never be found.

But on the third day, without anyone's saying, they felt the approach of a great presence.

It was the poet who finally put it in words:

"Is God humming under His breath somewhere?"

"What a fierce scum you are," said his wife. "Can't you speak plain English even when you gossip?"

"Damn it, listen!" cried the poet.

So they listened.

"Don't you feel as if you stood on the threshold of a giant blast-furnace kitchen, and inside somewhere, all comfortably warm, vast hands flour-gloved, smelling of wondrous tripes and miraculous viscera, bloodied and proud of the blood, somewhere

God cooks out the dinnertime of life? In that caldron sun, a brew to make the flowering forth of life on Venus, in that vat, a stew broth of bones and nervous heart to run in animals on planets ten billion light-years gone. And isn't God content at His fabulous workings in the great kitchen universe, where He has menu'd out a history of feasts, famines, deaths and reburgeonings for a billion billion years? And if God be content, would He not hum under His breath? Feel your bones. Aren't the marrows teeming with that hum? For that matter, God not only hums, He sings in the elements. He dances in molecules. Eternal celebration swarms us. Something is near. Sh."

He pressed his fat finger to his pouting lips.

And now all were silent, and Cara Corelli's paleness searchlighted the darkening waters ahead.

They all felt it. Wilder did. Parkhill did. They smoked to cover it. They put the smokes out. They waited in the dusk.

And the humming grew nearer. And the hunter, smelling it, went to join the silent actress at the bow of the yacht. And the poet sat to write down the words he had spoken.

"Yes," he said as the stars came out. "It's almost upon us. It has"—he took a breath—"arrived."

The yacht passed into a tunnel.

The tunnel went under a mountain.

And the City was there.

• • •

It was a city within a hollow mountain, with its own meadows surrounding it and its own strangely colored and illumined stone sky above it. And it had been lost and remained lost for the simple reason that people had tried flying to discover it or had unraveled roads to find it, when all the while the canals that led to it stood waiting for simple walkers to tread where once waters had trod.

And now the yacht filled with strange people from another planet touched an ancient wharf.

And the City stirred.

In the old days, cities were alive or dead if there were or were not people in them. It was that simple. But in the later days of life on Earth or Mars, cities did not die. They slept. And in their dreamful coggeries and enwheeled slumbers they remembered how once it was or how it might be again.

So as, one by one, the party filed out on the dock, they felt a great personage, the hidden, oiled, the metaled and shining soul of the metropolis slide in a landfall of muted and hidden fireworks toward becoming fully awake.

The weight of the new people on the dock caused a machined exhalation. They felt themselves on delicate scales. The dock sank a millionth of an inch.

And the City, the cumbrous Sleeping Beauty of a nightmare device, sensed this touch, this kiss, and slept no more.

Thunder.

In a wall 100 feet high stood a gate 70 feet wide. This gate, in two parts, now rumbled back to hide within the wall.

Aaronson stepped forward.

Wilder moved to intercept him. Aaronson sighed.

"Captain, no advice, please. No warnings. No patrols going on ahead to flush out villains. The City wants us in. It welcomes us. Surely you don't imagine anything's *alive* in there? It's a robot place. And don't look as if you think it's a time bomb. It hasn't seen fun and games in—what? Do you read Martian hieroglyphics? That cornerstone. The City was built at least twenty thousand years ago."

"And abandoned," said Wilder.

"You make it sound like a plague drove them——"

"Not a plague." Wilder stirred uneasily, feeling

himself weighed on the great scales beneath his feet. "Something. Something. . . ."

"Let's find out! In, all of you!"

Singly and in pairs, the people from Earth stepped over the threshold.

Wilder, last of all, stepped across.

And the City came more alive.

The metal roofs of the City sprang wide like the petals of a flower.

Windows flicked wide like the lids of vast eyes to stare down upon them.

A river of sidewalks gently purled and washed at their feet, machined creekways that gleamed off through the City.

Aaronson gazed at the metal tides with pleasure. "Well, by God, the burden's off me! I was going to picnic you all. But that's the City's business now. Meet you back here in two hours to compare notes! Here goes!"

And saying this, he leaped out onto the scurrying silver carpet that treaded him swiftly away.

Wilder, alarmed, moved to follow. But Aaronson cried jovially back:

"Come on in, the water's fine!"

And the metal river whisked him, waving, off.

And one by one they stepped forward and the moving sidewalk drifted them away. Parkhill, the hunter, the poet and his wife, the actor, and then the beautiful woman and her maid. They floated like statues mysteriously borne on volcanic fluids that swept them anywhere, or nowhere; they could only guess.

Wilder jumped. The river seized his boots gently. Following, he went away into the avenues and around the bends of parks and through fiords of buildings.

And behind them, the dock and the gate stood empty. There was no trace to show they had arrived. It was almost as if they had never been.

● ● ●

Beaumont, the actor, was the first to leave the traveling pathway. A certain building caught his eye. And the next thing he knew, he had leaped off and edged near, sniffing.

He smiled.

For now he knew what kind of building he stood before, because of the odor that drifted from it.

"Brass polish. And, by God, that means only one thing!"

Theater.

Brass doors, brass rails, brass rings on velvet curtains.

He opened the door of the building and stepped in. He sniffed and laughed aloud. Yes. Without a sign or a light, the smell alone, the special chemistry of metals and dust torn free of a million tickets.

And above all . . . he listened. The silence.

"The silence that waits. No other silence in the world waits. Only in a theater will you find that. The very particles of air chafe themselves in readiness. The shadows sit back and hold their breath. Well . . . ready or not . . . here I come. . . ."

The lobby was green velvet undersea.

The theater itself, red velvet undersea, only dimly perceived as he opened the double doors. Somewhere beyond was a stage.

Something shuddered like a great beast. His breath had dreamed it alive. The air from his half-opened mouth caused the curtains 100 feet away to softly furl and unfurl in darkness like all-covering wings.

Hesitantly, he took a step.

A light began to appear everywhere in a high ceiling where a school of miraculous prism fish swam upon themselves.

The oceanarium light played everywhere. He gasped.

The theater was full of people.

A thousand people sat motionless in the false dusk. True, they were small, fragile, rather dark, they wore silver masks, yet—people!

He knew, without asking, they had sat here for endless centuries.

Yet they were not dead.

They were—he reached out a hand. He tapped the wrist of a man seated on the aisle.

The hand tinkled quietly.

He touched the shoulder of a woman. She chimed. Like a bell.

Yes, they had waited some few thousand years. But then, machines have a property of waiting.

He took a further step and froze.

For a sigh had passed over the crowd.

It was like the sound, the first small sound a new-born babe must make in the moment before it really sucks, bleats and shocks out its wailing surprise at being alive.

A thousand such sighs faded in the velvet portieres.

Beneath the masks, hadn't a thousand mouths drifted ajar?

He moved. He stopped.

Two thousand eyes blinked wide in the velvet dusk.

He moved again.

A thousand silent heads wheeled on their ancient but well-oiled cogs.

They looked at him.

An unquenchable cold ran wild in him.

He turned to run.

But their eyes would not let him go.

And, from the orchestra pit, music.

He looked and saw, slowly rising, an insect agglomeration of instruments, all strange, all grotesquely acrobatic in their configurations. These were being softly thrummed, piped, touched and massaged in tune.

The audience, with a motion, turned their gaze to the stage.

A light flashed on. The orchestra struck a grand fanfare chord.

The red curtains parted. A spotlight fixed itself to front center, blazing upon an empty dais where sat an empty chair.

Beaumont waited.

No actor appeared.

A stir. Several hands were lifted to left and right. The hands came together. They beat softly in applause.

Now the spotlight wandered off the stage and up the aisle.

The heads of the audience turned to follow the empty ghost of light. The masks gleamed softly. The eyes behind the masks beckoned with warm color.

Beaumont stepped back.

But the light came steadily. It painted the floor with a blunt cone of pure whiteness.

And stopped, nibbling, at his feet.

The audience, turned, applauded even louder now. The theater banged, roared, ricocheted with their ceaseless tide of approbation.

Everything dissolved within him, from cold to warm. He felt as if he had been thrust raw into a downpour of summer rain. The storm rinsed him with gratitude. His heart jumped in great compulsive beats. His fists let go of themselves. His skeleton relaxed. He waited a moment longer, with the rain drenching over his upthrust and thankful cheeks and hammering his hungry eyelids so they fluttered to lock against themselves, and then he felt himself, like a ghost on battlements, led by a ghost light, lean, step, drift, move down and along the incline, sliding to beautiful ruin, now no longer walking but striding, not striding but in full-tilted run, and the masks glittering, the eyes hot with delight and fantastic welcoming, the flights of hands on the disturbed

air in upflung dove-winged rifle-shot flight. He felt
the steps collide with his shoes. The applause
slammed to a shutdown.

He swallowed. Then slowly he ascended the steps
and stood in the full light with a thousand masks
fixed to him and two thousand eyes watchful, and
he sat in the empty chair, and the theater grew
darker and the immense hearth-bellow breathing
softer out of the lyre-metal throats, and there was
only the sound of a mechanical beehive thrived
with machinery musk in the dark.

He held onto his knees. He let go. And at last
he spoke:

"To be or not to be——"

The silence was complete.

Not a cough. Not a stir. Not a rustle. Not a blink.
All waited. Perfection. The perfect audience. Perfect, forever and forever. Perfect. Perfect.

He tossed his words slowly into that perfect pond
and felt the soundless ripples disperse and gentle
away.

"——that is the question."

He talked. They listened. He knew that they
would never let him go now. They would beat him
insensible with applause. He would sleep a child's
sleep and arise to speak again. All of Shakespeare, all
of Shaw, all of Molière, every bit, crumb, lump,
joint and piece. *Himself* in repertory!

He arose to finish.

Finished, he thought. Bury me! Cover me!
Smother me deep!

Obediently, the avalanche came down the mountain.

• • •

Cara Corelli found a palace of mirrors.

The maid remained outside.

And Cara Corelli went in.

As she walked through a maze, the mirrors took

away a day, and then a week, and then a month
and then a year and then two years of time from
her face.

It was a palace of splendid and soothing lies. It
was like being young once more. It was being surrounded by all those tall, bright glass mirror men
who would never again in your life tell you the
truth.

Cara walked to the center of the palace. By the
time she stopped, she saw herself 25 years old in
every tall, bright mirror face.

She sat down in the middle of the bright maze.
She beamed around in happiness.

The maid waited outside for perhaps an hour.
And then she went away.

●   ●   ●

This was a dark place with shapes and sizes as
yet unseen. It smelled of lubricating oil, the blood
of tyrant lizards with cogs and wheels for teeth,
which lay strewn and silent in the dark, waiting.

A titan's door slowly gave a slithering roar, like a
backswept armored tail, and Parkhill stood in the
rich, oily wind blowing out around him. He felt as
if someone had pasted a white flower on his face.
But it was only a sudden surprise of a smile.

His empty hands hung at his sides and they made
impulsive and completely unconscious gestures forward. They beggared the air. So, paddling silently,
he let himself be moved into the garage, machine
shop, repair shed, whatever it was.

And, filled with holy delight and a child's holy
and unholy glee at what he beheld, he walked and
slowly turned.

For as far as his eye could see stood vehicles.

Vehicles that ran on the earth. Vehicles that flew
in the air. Vehicles that stood ready with wheels
to go in any direction. Vehicles with two wheels.
Vehicles with three or four or six or eight. Vehicles

that looked like butterflies. Vehicles that resembled ancient motor bikes. Three thousand stood ranked here, four thousand glinted ready there. Another thousand were tilted over, wheels off, copper guts exposed, waiting to be repaired. Still another thousand were lifted high on spidery repair hoists, their lovely undersides revealed to view, their disks and tubes and coggeries all intricate and fine and needful of touching, unbolting, revalving, rewiring, oiling, delicate lubricating. . . .

Parkhill's palms itched.

He walked forward through the primeval smell of swamp oils among the dead-and-waiting-to-be-revived ancient-but-new armored mechanical reptiles, and the more he looked the more he ached his grin.

The City was a city all right and, to a point, self-sustaining. But, eventually, the rarest butterflies of metal gossamer, gaseous oil and fiery dream sank to earth, the machines that repaired the machines that repaired the machines grew old, ill and damaging of themselves. Here, then, was the bestial garage, the slumberous elephant's bone yard where the aluminum dragons crawled rusting out their souls, hopeful of one live person left among so much active-but-dead metal, that person to put things right. One god of the machines to say, you Lazarus-elevator, rise up! You hovercraft, be reborn! And anoint them with leviathan oils, tap them with magical wrench and send them forth to almost eternal lives in and on the air and above the quicksilver paths.

Parkhill moved among 900 robot men and women slaughtered by simple corrosion. He would cure their rust.

Now. If he started now, thought Parkhill, rolling up his sleeves and staring off down a corridor of machines that ran waiting for a solid mile of garage, shed, hoist, lift, storage bin, oil tank and strewn shrapnel of tools glittering and ready for his grip;

if he started now, he might work his way to the end of the giant's ever-constant garage, accident, collision and repair-works shed in 30 years!

A billion bolts to be tightened. A billion motors to be tinkered! A billion gross anatomical mysteries to lie under, a grand oil-dripped-upon orphan, alone, alone, alone with the always-beautiful and never-talking-back hummingbird-commotion devices, accouterments and miraculous contraptions.

His hands weighed him toward the tools. He clutched a wrench. He found a 40-wheeled low running sled. He lay down on it. He sculled the garage in a long whistling ride. The sled scuttled.

Parkhill vanished beneath a great car of some ancient design.

Out of sight, you could hear him working on the gut of the machine. On his back, he talked up at it. And when he slapped it to life, at last, the machine talked back.

• • •

Always the silver pathways ran somewhere.

Thousands of years now they had run empty, carrying only dust to destinations away and away among the high and dreaming buildings.

Now, on one traveling path, Aaronson came borne like an aging statue.

And the more the road propelled him, the faster the City exposed itself to his view; the more buildings that passed, the more parks that sprang into sight, the more his smile faded. His color changed.

"Toy," he heard himself whisper. The whisper was ancient. "Just another"—and here his voice grew so small it faded away—"another toy."

A supertoy, yes. But his life was full of such and had always been so. If it was not some slot machine, it was the next-size dispenser or a jumbo-size razzmatazz hi-fi stereo speaker. From a lifetime of handling metallic sandpaper, he felt his arms rubbed away to a nub. Mere pips, his fingers. No, handless and lacking wrists. Aaronson, the Seal Boy!!! His mindless flippers clapped applause to a city that was, in reality, no more and no less than an economy-size jukebox ravening under its idiot breath. And—he knew the tune! God help him. He *knew* the tune.

He blinked just once.

An inner eyelid came down like cold glass.

He turned and trod the silver waters of the path.

He found a moving river of steel to take him back toward the great gate itself.

On the way, he met Cara Corelli's maid, wandering lost on her own silver stream.

• • •

As for the poet and his wife, their running battle tore echoes everywhere. They cried down 30 avenues, cracked panes in 200 shops, battered leaves from 70 varieties of park bush and tree, and only ceased when drowned by a thundering fountain display they passed, like a rise of clear fireworks upon the metropolitan air.

"The whole thing is," said his wife, punctuating one of his dirtier responses, "you only came along so you could lay hands on the nearest woman and spray her ears with bad breath and worse poetry."

The poet muttered a foul word.

"You're worse than the actor," said his wife. "Always at it. Don't you ever shut up?"

"Don't you?" he cried. "Ah, God, I've curdled inside. Shut up, woman, or I'll throw myself in the founts!"

"No. You haven't bathed in years. You're the pig of the century! Your picture will grace the *Swine Herder's Annual* next month!"

"That *did* it!"

Doors slammed on a building.

By the time she got off and ran back and fisted the doors, they were locked.

"Coward!" she shrieked. "Open up!"

A foul word came echoing out dimly.

•   •   •

"Ah, listen to that sweet silence," he whispered to himself in the great shelled dark.

Harpwell found himself in a soothing hugeness, a vast womblike building, over which hung a canopy of pure serenity, a starless void.

In the middle of this room, which was roughly a 200-foot circle, stood a device, a machine. In this machine were dials and rheostats and switches, a seat and a steering wheel.

"What kind of junk is this?" whispered the poet, but edged near and bent to touch. "Christ-off-the-cross and bearing mercy, it smells of what? Blood and mere guts? No, for it's clean as a virgin's frock. Still, it does fill the nose. Violence. Simple destruction. I can feel the damn carcass tremble like a nervous highbred hound. It's full of *stuffs*. Let's try a swig."

He sat in the machine.

"What do I twig first? This?"

He snapped a switch.

The Baskerville-hound machine whimpered in its dog slumberings.

"Good beast." He flicked another switch. "How do you go, brute? When the damn device is in full tilt, where to? You lack wheels. Well, surprise me. I dare."

The machine shivered.

The machine bolted.

It ran. It dashed.

He held tight to the steering wheel.

"Holy God!"

For he was on a highway, racing fast.

Air sluiced by. The sky flashed over in running colors.

The speedometer read 70, 80.

And the highway ribboned away ahead, flashing toward him. Invisible wheels slapped and banged on an increasingly rough road.

Far away, ahead, a car appeared.

It was running fast. And——

"It's on the wrong side of the road! Do you see that, wife? The wrong side."

Then he realized his wife was not here.

He was alone in a car racing—90 miles an hour now—toward another car racing at a similar speed.

He veered the wheel.

His vehicle moved to the left.

Almost instantly, the other car did a compensating move and ran back over to the left.

"The damn fool, what does he think—where's the blasted brake?"

He stomped the floor. There was no brake. Here was a strange machine indeed. One that ran as fast as you wished, but never stopped until what?—it ran itself down? There was no brake. Nothing but— further accelerators. A whole series of round buttons on the floor, which, as he tromped them, surged power into the motor.

Ninety, 100, 120 miles an hour.

"God in heaven!" he screamed. "We're going to hit! How do you like that, girl?"

And in the last instant before collision, he imagined she rather liked it fine.

The cars hit. They erupted in gaseous flame. They burst apart in flinders. They tumbled. He felt himself jerked now this way, now that. He was a torch hurtled skyward. His arms and legs danced a crazy rigadoon in mid-air as he felt his peppermint-stick bones snap in brittle and agonizing ecstasies. Then, clutching death as a dark mate, gesticulating, he fell away in a black surprise, drifting toward further nothings.

He lay dead.

He lay dead a long while.

Then he opened one eye.

He felt the slow burner under his soul. He felt the bubbled water rising to the top of his mind like tea brewing.

"I'm dead," he said, "but alive. Did you see all that, wife? Dead but alive."

He found himself sitting in the vehicle, upright.

He sat there for ten minutes thinking about all that had happened.

"Well, now," he mused. "Was that not interesting? Not to say fascinating? Not to say almost exhilarating? I mean, sure, it knocked the stuff out of me, scared the soul out one ear and back the other, hit my wind and tore my seams, broke the bones and shook the wits, but, but, but, wife, but, but, but, dear sweet Meg, Meggy, Megeen, I wish you were here; it might tamp the tobacco tars out of your half-ass lungs and bray the mossy-graveyard back-breaking meanness from your marrow. Let me see here, now, wife; let's have a look, Harpwell-my-husband-the-poet."

He tinkered with the dials.

He thrummed the great hound motor.

"Shall we chance another diversion? Try another embattled picnic excursion? Let's."

And he set the car on its way.

Almost immediately, the vehicle was traveling 100 and then 150 miles per hour.

Almost immediately, an opposing car appeared ahead on the wrong side of the road.

"Death," said the poet. "Are you always here, then? Do you hang about? Is this your questing place? Let's test your mettle!"

The car raced. The opposing car hurtled.

He wheeled over into the far-left lane.

The opposing car shifted, homing toward Destroy.

"Yes, I see; well, then, this," said the poet.

And switched a switch and jumped another throttle.

In the instant before impact, the two cars transformed themselves. Shuttering through illusory veils, they became jetcraft at take-off. Shrieking, the two jets banged flame, tore air, yammered back soundbarrier explosions before the mightiest one of all—as the two bullets impacted, fused, interwove, interlaced blood, mind and eternal blackness, and fell away into a net of strange and peaceful midnight.

I'm dead, he thought again.

And it feels fine, thanks.

He awoke at the touch of his own smile.

He was seated in the vehicle.

Twice dead, he thought, and feeling better each time. Why? Isn't that odd? Curiouser and curiouser. Queer beyond queerness.

He thrummed the motor again.

What this time?

Does it locomote? he wondered. How about a big black choo-choo train out of half-primordial times?

And he was on his way, an engineer. The sky flicked over, and the motion-picture screens or whatever they were pressed in with swift illusions of pouring smoke and steaming whistle and huge wheel within wheel on grinding track, and the track ahead wound through hills, and far on up around a mountain came another train, black as a buffalo herd, pouring belches of smoke, on the same two rails, the same track, heading toward wondrous accident.

"I see," said the poet. "I do begin to see. I begin to know what this is used for—for such as me, the poor wandering idiots of a world, confused and sore put-upon by mothers as soon as dropped from wombs, insulted with Christian guilt and gone mad from the need of destruction, and collecting a pittance of hurt here and scar tissue there, and a larger, portable wife grievance beyond; but one thing sure, we do want to die, we do want to be killed, and here's the very thing for it, in convenient quick pay! So pay it out, machine; dole it out, sweet, raving device! Rape away, death! I'm your very man."

And the two locomotives met and climbed each other. Up a black ladder of explosion they wheeled and locked their drive shafts and plastered their slick negro bellies together and rubbed boilers and beautifully banged the night in a single outflung whirl and flurry of meteor and flame. Then the locomotives, in a cumbrous rapine dance, seized and melted together with their violence and passion, gave a monstrous curtsy and fell off the mountain and took a thousand years to go all the way down to the rocky pits.

The poet awoke and immediately grabbed the controls. He was humming under his breath, stunned. He was singing wild tunes. His eyes flashed. His heart beat swiftly.

"More, more. I see it now, I know what to do. More, more, please, O God, more, for the truth shall set me free, more!"

He hoofed three, four, five pedals.

He snapped six switches.

The vehicle was auto-jet-locomotive-glider-missile-rocket.

He ran, he steamed, he roared, he soared, he flew. Cars veered toward him. Locomotives loomed. Jets rammed. Rockets screamed.

And in one wild three-hour spree he hit 200 cars, rammed 20 trains, blew up 10 gliders, exploded 40 missiles, and, far out in space, gave up his glorious soul in a final Fourth-of-July death celebration as an interplanetary rocket going 200,000 miles an hour struck an iron planetoid and went beautifully to hell.

In all, in a few short hours he figured he must have been torn apart and put back together a few times less than 500.

When it was all over, he sat not touching the wheel, his feet free of the pedals.

After a half hour of sitting there, he began to laugh. He threw his head back and let out great war whoops. Then he got up, shaking his head, drunker than ever in his life, really drunk now, and he knew he would stay that way forever and never need drink again.

I'm punished, he thought, really punished at last. Really hurt at last, and hurt enough, over and over, so I will never need hurt again, never need to be destroyed again, never have to collect another insult or take another wound, or ask for a simple grievance. God bless the genius of man and the inventors of such machines, that enable the guilty to pay and at last be rid of the dark albatross and the awful burden. Thank you, City; thank you, old blueprinter of needful souls. Thank you. And which way out?

A door slid open.

His wife stood waiting for him.

"Well, there you are," she said. "And still drunk."

"No," he said. "Dead."

"Drunk."

"Dead," he said, "beautifully dead at last. Which means free. I won't need you anymore, dead Meg-Meggy-Megeen. You're set free, also, like an awful conscience. Go haunt someone else, girl. Go destroy. I forgive you your sins on me, for I have at last forgiven myself. I am off the Christian hook. I am the dear wandering dead who, dead, can at last live. Go and do likewise, lady. Inside with you. Be punished and set free. So long, Meg, so long. Farewell. Toodleoo."

He wandered away.

"Where do you think you're going?" she cried.

"Why, out into life and the blood of life, and
happy at last."

"Come back here!" she screamed.

"You can't stop the dead, for they wander the
universe, happy as children in the dark field."

"Harpwell!" she brayed. "Harpwell!"

But he stepped on a river of silver metal.

And let the dear river bear him, laughing until the
tears glittered on his cheeks, away and away from
the shriek and the bray and the scream of that
woman—what was her name?—no matter, back there
and gone.

And when he reached the gate, he walked out
and along the canal in the fine day, heading toward
the far towns.

By that time, he was singing every old tune he had
known as a child of six. . . .

Behind him, by the strange building that had set
him free, his wife stood a long while staring at the
metal path that had floated him away. Then slowly
she turned to glare at the enemy building. She fisted
the door once. It slid open, waiting. She sniffed.
She scowled at the interior.

Then, steadily, hands ready to seize and grapple,
she advanced. With each step she grew bolder. Her
face thrust like an ax at the strange air.

Behind her, unnoticed, the door closed.

It did not open again.

• • •

It was a church.

It was not a church.

Wilder let the door swing shut.

He stood in cathedral darkness, waiting.

The roof, if roof there was, breathed up in a great
suspense, flowed up beyond reach or sight.

The floor, if floor there was, was a mere firmness
beneath. It, too, was black.

And then the stars came out. It was like that first

night of childhood when his father had taken him out beyond the city to a hill where the streetlights could not diminish the universe. And there were a thousand, no ten thousand, no ten million billion stars filling the darkness. The stars were manifold and bright, and they did not care. Even then he had known: They do not care. If I breathe or do not breathe, live or die, the eyes that look from all around don't care. And he had seized his father's hand and gripped tight, as if he might fall up into that abyss.

Now, in this building, he was full of the old terror and the old sense of beauty and the old silent crying out after mankind. The stars filled him with pity for small men lost in so much size.

Then yet another thing happened:

Beneath his feet, space opened wide and let through yet another billion sparks of light.

He was suspended as a fly is held upon a vast telescopic lens. He walked on a water of space. He stood upon a transparent flex of great eye, and all about him, as on a night in winter, beneath foot and above head, in all directions, were nothing but stars.

So, in the end, it was a church, it was a cathedral, a multitude of far-flung universal shrines, here a worshiping of Horsehead Nebula, there Orion's galaxy, and there Andromeda, like the head of God, fiercely gazed and thrust through the raw dark stuffs of night to stab his soul and pin it writhing against the backside of his flesh.

God, everywhere, fixed him with shutterless and unblinking eyes.

And he, a bacterial shard of that same Flesh, stared back and winced but the slightest.

He waited. And a planet drifted upon the void. It spun by once with a great mellow autumn face. It circled and came under him.

And he stood upon a far world of green grass and

great lush trees, where the air was fresh and a
river ran by like the rivers of childhood, flashing
the sun and leaping with fish.

He knew that he had traveled very far to reach
this world. Behind him lay the rocket. Behind lay
a century of travel, of sleeping, of waiting, and
now, here was the reward.

"Mine?" he asked the simple air, the simple grass,
the long simplicity of water that spilled by in the
shallow sands.

And the world answered, wordless: Yours.

Yours without the long travel and the boredom,
yours without 99 years of flight from Earth, of
sleeping in kept tubes, of intravenous feedings, of
nightmares dreamed of Earth lost and gone, yours
without torture, without pain, yours without trial
and error, failure and destruction. Yours without
sweat and terror. Yours without a falling down of
tears. Yours. Yours.

But Wilder did not put out his hands to accept.

And the sun dimmed in the alien sky.

And the world drifted from under his feet.

And yet another world swam up and passed in a
huge parade of even brighter glories.

And this world, too, spun up to take his weight.
And here, if anything, the fields were richer green,
the mountains capped with melting snows, far fields
ripening with strange harvests, and scythes waiting
on the edge of fields for him to lift and sweep and
cut the grain and live out his life any way that he
might.

Yours. The merest touch of weather upon the
hairs within his ear said this. Yours.

And Wilder, without shaking his head, moved
back. He did not say no. He thought his rejection.

And the grass died in the fields.

The mountains crumbled.

The river shallows ran to dust.

And the world sprang away.

And Wilder stood again in space where God had stood before creating a world out of chaos.

And at last he spoke and said to himself:

"It would be easy. Oh, Lord, yes, I'd like that. No work, nothing, just accept. But . . . You can't *give* me what I want."

He looked at the stars.

"Nothing can be given, ever."

The stars were growing dim.

"It's really very simple. I must borrow, I must earn. I must take."

The stars quivered and died.

"Much obliged and thank you, no."

The stars were all gone.

He turned and, without looking back, walked upon darkness. He hit the door with his palm. He strode out into the City.

He refused to hear if the machine universe behind him cried out in a great chorus, all cries and wounds, like a woman scorned. The crockery in a vast robot kitchen fell. By the time it hit the floor, he was gone.

● ● ●

It was a museum of weapons.

The hunter walked among the cases.

He opened a case and hefted a weapon constructed like a spider's antennae.

It hummed, and a flight of metal bees sizzled out the rifle bore, flew away and stung a target-man-mannequin some 50 yards away, then fell lifeless, clattering to the floor.

The hunter nodded with admiration and put the rifle back in the case.

He prowled on, curious as a child, testing yet other weapons here and there that dissolved glass or caused metal to run in bright yellow pools of molten lava.

"Excellent! Fine! Absolutely great!"

His cry rang out again and again as he slammed cases open and shut and finally chose the gun.

It was a gun that, without fuss or fury, did away with matter. You pressed the button, there was a brief discharge of blue light and the target simply vanished. No blood. No bright lava. No trace.

"All right," he announced, leaving the place of guns, "we have the weapon. How about the game, the grandest beast ever in the long hunt?"

He leaped onto the moving sidewalk.

An hour later he had passed a thousand buildings and scanned a thousand open parks without itching his finger.

He moved uneasily from treadway to treadway, shifting speeds now in this direction, now in that.

Until at last he saw a river of metal that sped underground.

Instinctively, he jumped toward that.

The metal stream carried him down into the secret gut of the City.

Here all was warm blood darkness. Here strange pumps moved the pulse of the City. Here were distilled the sweats that lubricated the roadways and lifted the elevators and swarmed the offices and stores with motion.

The hunter half crouched on the roadway. His eyes squinted. Perspiration gathered in his palms. His trigger finger greased the metal gun, sliding.

"Yes," he whispered. "By God, now. This is it. The City itself . . . the great beast. Why didn't I think of that? The animal City, the dread carnivore that has men for breakfast, lunch and dinner; it kills them with machines, it munches their bones like bread sticks, it spits them out like toothpicks, and it lives long after they die. The City, by God, the City. Well, now. . . ."

He glided through dark grottoes of television eyes that showed him remote parkways and high towers.

Deeper within the belly of the underground world he sank as the river lowered itself. He passed a school of computers that chattered in maniac chorus. He shuddered as a cloud of paper confetti from one titan machine, holes punched out to perhaps record his passing, fell upon him in a whispered snow.

He raised his gun. He fired.

The machine disappeared.

He fired again. A skeleton strutwork under yet another machine vanished.

The City screamed.

At first very low and then very high, then, rising, falling, like a siren. Lights flashed. Bells began to ricochet alarms. The metal river shuddered under his feet. He fired at television screens that glared all white upon him. They blinked out and did not exist.

The City screamed higher until he raved against it himself.

He did not see, until it was too late, that the road on which he sped fell into the gnashing maw of a machine that was used for some purpose long-forgotten centuries before.

He thought that by pressing the trigger he would make the terrible mouth disappear. It did indeed vanish. But as the roadway sped on and he whirled and fell as it picked up speed, he realized at last that his weapon did not truly destroy; it merely made invisible what was there and what still remained, though unseen.

He gave a terrible cry to match the cry of the City. He flung out the gun in a last blow. The gun went into cogs and wheels and teeth and was twisted down.

The last thing he saw was a deep elevator shaft that fell away for perhaps a mile into the earth.

He knew that it might take him two minutes to hit the bottom. He shrieked.

The worst thing was, he would be conscious . . .
all the way down. . . .

• • •

The rivers shook. The silver rivers trembled. The
pathways, shocked, convulsed the metal shores
through which they sped.

Wilder, traveling, was almost knocked flat by the
concussion.

What had caused the concussion he could not see.
Perhaps, far off, there was a cry, a murmur of dread-
ful sound, which swiftly faded.

Wilder moved. The silver track threaded on.
But the City seemed poised, agape. The City seemed
tensed. Its huge and various muscles were cramped,
alert.

Feeling this, Wilder began to walk as well as be
moved by the swift path.

"Thank God. There's the gate. The sooner I'm
out of this place, the happier I'll——"

The gate was indeed there, not a hundred yards
away. But, on the instant, as if hearing his declara-
tion, the river stopped. It shivered. Then it started
to move back, taking him where he did not wish
to go.

Incredulous, Wilder spun about and, in spinning,
fell. He clutched at the stuffs of the rushing sidewalk.

His face, pressed to the vibrant grillwork of the
river-rushing pavement, heard the machineries mesh
and mill beneath, humming and agroan, forever
sluicing, forever feverish for journeys and mindless
excursions. Beneath the calm metal, embattlements
of hornets stung and buzzed, lost bees bumbled and
subsided. Collapsed, he saw the gate lost away
behind. Burdened, he remembered at last the extra
weight upon his back, the jet-power equipment that
might give him wings.

He jammed his hand to the switch on his belt.

And in the instant before the sidewalk might have pulsed him off among sheds and museum walls, he was airborne.

Flying, he hovered, then swam the air back to hang above a casual Parkhill gazing up, all covered with grease and smiling from a dirty face. Beyond Parkhill, at the gate, stood the frightened maid. Beyond even farther, near the yacht at the landing, stood Aaronson, his back turned to the City, nervous to be moving on.

"Where are the others?" cried Wilder.

"Oh, they won't be back," said Parkhill easily. "It figures, doesn't it? I mean, it's quite a place."

"Place!" said Wilder, hovered now up, now down, turning slowly, apprehensive. "We've got to get them out! It's not safe."

"It's safe if you like it. I like it," said Parkhill.

And all the while there was a gathering of earthquake in the ground and in the air, which Parkhill chose to ignore.

"You're leaving, of course," he said, as if nothing were wrong. "I knew you would. Why?"

"Why?" Wilder wheeled like a dragonfly before a trembling of storm wind. Buffeted up, buffeted down, he flung his words at Parkhill, who didn't bother to duck but smiled up and accepted. "Good God, Sam, the place is hell. The Martians had enough sense to get out. They saw they had overbuilt themselves. The damn City does everything, which is too much! Sam!"

And at that instant, they both looked round and up. For the sky was shelling over. Great lids were vising in the ceiling. Like an immense flower, the tops of buildings were petaling out to cover themselves. Windows were shutting down. Doors were slamming. A sound of fired cannons echoed through the streets.

The gate was thundering shut.

The twin jaws of the gate, shuddering, were in motion.

Wilder cried out, spun around and dived.

He heard the maid below him. He saw her reach up. Then, swooping, he gathered her in. He kicked the air. The jet lifted them both.

Like a bullet to a target, he rammed for the gate. But an instant before he reached it, burdened, the gates banged together. He was barely able to veer course and soar upward along the raw metal as the entire City shook with the roar of the steel.

Parkhill shouted below. And Wilder was flying up, up along the wall, looking this way and that.

Everywhere, the sky was closing in. The petals were coming down, coming down. There was only a last small patch of stone sky to his right. He blasted for that. And kicking, made it through, flying, as the final flange of steel clipped into place and the City was closed to itself.

He hung for a moment, suspended, and then flew with the woman down along the outer wall to the dock, where Aaronson stood by the yacht staring at the huge shut gates.

"Parkhill," whispered Wilder, looking at the City, the walls, the gates. "You fool. You damned fool."

"Fools, all of them," said Aaronson and turned away. "Fools. Fools."

They waited a moment longer and listened to the City, humming, alive, kept to itself, its great mouth filled with a few bits of warmth, a few lost people somewhere hid away in there. The gates would stay shut now, forever. The City had what it needed to go on a long while.

Wilder looked back at the place as the yacht took them back out of the mountain and away up the canal.

They passed the poet a mile farther on, walking along the rim of the canal. He waved them off. "No.

No, thanks. I feel like walking. It's a fine day. Good-bye. Go on."

The towns lay ahead. Small towns. Small enough to be run by men instead of the towns running them. He heard the brass music. He saw the neon lights at dusk. He made out the junk yards in the fresh night under the stars.

Beyond the towns stood the silver rockets, tall, waiting to be fired off and away toward the wilderness of stars.

"Real," whispered the rockets, "real stuff. Real travel. Real time. Real space. No gifts. Nothing free. Just a lot of good brute work."

The yacht touched into its home dock.

"Rockets, by God," he murmured. "Wait till I get my hands on you."

He ran off in the night to do just that.

December 28th

theodore l. thomas

Why must they do it on December 28th? John
Stapleton considered the question. That was the
worst part of it, the date. December 28th, tucked
neatly between the brightest holidays of the year.

Stapleton spun from the small window in a char-
acteristic rush of motion. Hands locked behind him,
he stared at the door. In the back of his mind he
knew there was a good reason for the date. They
had picked the anniversary of the day he and Ardelle
had married, a day of special gladness, in the heart
of the holiday season. Yes, December 28th was a
time for many things, but it was not a time for a
hanging.

In three steps Stapleton was at the door; he
took the bars into his two great hands. Understand-
ing the reason for the date did nothing to sap his
anger at all. Most of the world celebrated, and it
seemed to Stapleton that this universal jubilee was
at his expense. The world danced at his hanging.

Stapleton somberly began his exercises. The
guards saw and looked at each other uncomfortably.
Stapleton took the pencil-thin bars into his two
hands and methodically tried to pull them apart.
First, the right hand directly in front of the massive

chest, the left hand off to one side. The tendons stretched audibly. Then the hands were reversed, and again the tightening of great muscles. Then both hands on a single bar and both feet on another. The soft grunts and the low rumbles deep in the throat echoed in the chamber as Stapleton worked on the bars, worked until his body was covered with a fine sweat. Stapleton knew, and the guards knew, that the thin shafts were of an alloy capable of withstanding the best efforts of ten men such as Stapleton. Yet the slow and careful straining, the deliberate and intense attack on the bars by the massive man created the illusion that he was able to rip them out of their moorings. Twice a day Stapleton took his exercises on the bars, and twice a day the guards watched with a fear that knowledge could not dispel.

Stapleton finished. He stood at the door breathing deeply, his hands clenching and unclenching, the fingers making a scraping sound as he forced the tips across the callused and furrowed palms. The guards visibly relaxed and turned away. Stapleton looked at the clock and grunted. It was almost time. In a few moments now, they would come for him.

He grunted louder. Let them come. Ardelle was dead, Ardelle and that other. And no matter what they said or did, it was right it should be that way. There are things a man knows who has been one with a woman like Ardelle. Between such a man and such a woman there could be nothing concealed, not for long. How strange that she should have tried.

But the time came when he looked at her with a mild question in his eyes. The response—the incredible, soul-shaking response—was a flicker of the panic of discovery. Just a brief flash in her eyes, but he read it well; it was enough.

Ardelle was silent throughout all that followed. She understood this man of iron and fire, and so through it all she made no sound, no moan. With the other it was different. The other had been playing a kind of game, and he was not at all prepared to pay the price of losing. He died badly.

And Stapleton? There was an enigma. Here and now, when men need no longer die for their crimes, was a man who refused to admit that a crime had been committed. So little was needed to save him, but that little he refused to give. Here and now, a man need only cry out, "Forgive me, I was wrong. Forgive me," and he was saved.

Stapleton turned to watch as the outer door opened to admit a tall gray-haired man. With measured strides, the man came close to the bars and looked through at Stapleton. The pain was as strong in his face as ever, the sorrow and pleading as eloquent. His words when he spoke were husky with suffering. "John Stapleton, how say you? Have you erred?"

Stapleton looked at him and said, "I have not erred. I did what had to be done, nothing more."

The man with the gray hair turned away. The walk back to the door was solemn, for his head was bent and his shoulders trembled. Then he was gone.

There was a stirring and a shuffling of many feet outside the outer door. Stapleton knew they were coming for him, and he stepped back to the center of the cell. He knew how this would be. They would come into his cell fearful that he would unleash his physical might; yet they would be unable to look at him. He would wait a moment, then laugh, then lead the procession to the gallows chamber. He would stand with his head in the enfolding blackness, feeling the snug rope around his throat and the knot behind his left ear. When the moment came, there would be no sensation of falling; there would be a mere lightening of pressure against his feet. And the thudding shock and the searing flash of light. Then blackness.

These things he knew well, but there were other things. There was the doctor who stood by to pronounce him dead at the earliest possible moment; the oxygen-carrying blood must not be kept from the brain longer than 4.3 minutes. Once dead, the intravenous needles were inserted and the pumps took over where the heart had failed.

The surgeons came on next. With high dexterity they repaired the broken cervical vertebra, the torn muscles, the crushed veins and arteries. When they were finished, they placed the head and neck in a cast and turned their attention to the restoration of the heartbeat. This was soon accomplished and, unconscious, Stapleton was wheeled to his cell.

Usually he recovered consciousness during the middle of January. By March he was out of bed, still wearing his cast. In June he started his exercises, for he insisted on being strong. In August he put aside his cast. All during the fall he grew strong in order that the cycle might begin again on December 28th. How many times had it been since that first time back in 1997? Fourteen? Eighteen? One loses count, but no matter. If this is what they must do, let them.

But why must they always do it on December 28th?

Who Shall Dwell...

h. c. neal

It came on a Sunday afternoon and that was good, because if it had happened on a weekday, the father would have been at work and the children at school, leaving the mother at home alone and the whole family disorganized with hardly any hope at all. They had prayed that it would never come, ever, but suddenly here it was.

The father, a slender, young-old man, slightly stooped from years of labor, was resting on the divan and half listening to a program of waltz music on the radio. Mother was in the kitchen preparing a chicken for dinner, and the younger boy and the girl were in the bedroom drawing crude pictures of familiar barnyard animals on a shared slate. The older boy was in the tack shed out back, saddle-soaping some harnesses.

When the waltz program was interrupted by an announcer with a routine political appeal, the father rose, tapped the ash from his pipe and ambled lazily into the kitchen.

"How about joining me in a little glass of wine?" he asked, patting his wife affectionately on the hip.

"If you don't think it would be too crowded," she replied, smiling easily at their standing jest.

154

He grinned amiably and reached into the cupboard for the bottle and glasses.

Suddenly the radio message was abruptly cut off. A moment of humming silence. Then, in a voice pregnant with barely controlled excitement, the announcer almost shouted:

"Bomb alert! Bomb alert! Attention! Attention! A salvo of missiles has just been launched across the sea, heading this way. Attention! They are expected to strike within the next sixteen minutes. Sixteen minutes! This is a verified alert! Take cover! Take cover! Keep your radios tuned for further instructions."

"My God!" the father gasped, dropping the glasses. "Oh, my God!" His ruggedly handsome face was ashen, puzzled, as though he knew beyond a shadow of doubt that this was real—but still could not quite believe it.

"Get the children," his wife blurted, then dashed to the door to call the older boy. He stared at her a brief moment, seeing the fear in her pretty face, but something else, too, something divorced from the fear. Defiance. And a loathing for all men involved in the making and dispatch of nuclear weapons.

He wheeled then and ran to the bedroom. "Let's go," he snapped, "shelter drill!" Despite a belated attempt to tone down the second phrase and make it seem like just another of the many rehearsals they'd had, his voice and bearing galvanized the youngsters into instant action. They leaped from the bed without a word and dashed for the door.

He hustled them through the kitchen to the rear door and sent them scooting to the shelter. As he returned to the bedroom for outer garments for himself and his wife, the older boy came running in.

"This is the hot one, son," said his father tersely, "the real one." He and the boy stared at each other a long moment, both knowing what must be done and each knowing the other would more than do his share, yet wondering still at the frightening fact that it must be done at all.

"How much time we got, dad?"

"Not long," the father replied, glancing at his watch, "twelve, maybe fourteen minutes."

The boy disappeared into the front room, going after the flashlight and battery radio. The father stepped to the closet, slid the door open and picked up the flat metal box containing their vital papers, marriage license, birth certificates, etc. He tossed the box on the bed, then took down his wife's short-coat and his own hunting jacket. Draping the clothing over his arm, he then picked up the metal box and the big family Bible from the headboard on the bed. Everything else they would need had been stored in the shelter the past several months. He heard his wife approaching and turned as she entered the room.

"Ready, dear?" she asked.

"Yes, we're ready now," he replied. "Have the kids gone in?"

"They're all down," she answered, then added with a faint touch of despairing bewilderment, "I still can't believe it's real."

"We've got to believe it," he said, looking her steadily in the eye. "We can't afford not to."

Outside, the day was crisp and clear, typical of early fall. Just right for boating on the river, fishing or bird shooting. A regular peach of a day, he thought, for fleeing underground to escape the awesome hell of a nuclear strike. Who was the writer who had said about atomic weapons, "Would any self-respecting cannibal toss one into a village of women and children?" He looked at his watch again. Four minutes had elapsed since the first alarm. Twelve minutes, more or less, remained.

Inside the shelter, he dogged the door with its

double-strength strap-iron bar and looked around to see that his family was squared away. His wife, wearing her attractive blue-print cotton frock (he noticed for the first time), was methodically checking the food supplies, assisted by the older son. The small children had already put their initial fright behind them, as is the nature of youngsters, and were drawing on the slate again in quiet, busy glee.

Now it began. The waiting.

They knew, the man and his wife, that others would come soon, begging and crying to be taken in now that the time was here, now that Armageddon had come screaming toward them, stabbing through the sky on stubbed wings of shining steel.

They had argued the aspects of this when the shelter was abuilding. It was in her mind to share their refuge. "We can't call ourselves Christians and then deny safety to our friends when the showdown comes," she contended. "That isn't what God teaches."

"That's nothing but religious pap," he retorted with a degree of anger, "oatmeal Christianity." For he was a hardheaded man, an Old Testament man. "God created the family as the basic unit of society," he reasoned. "That should make it plain that a man's primary Christian duty is to protect his family."

"But don't you see?" she protested. "We must prepare to purify ourselves . . . to rise above this 'mine' thinking and be as God's own Son, who said, 'Love thy neighbor.' "

"No," he replied with finality, "I can't buy that." Then, after a moment's thought while he groped for the words to make her understand the truth which burned in the core of his soul, "It is my family I must save, no one more. You. These kids. Our friends are like the people of Noah's time. He warned them of the coming flood when he built the ark on God's command. He was ridiculed and scoffed

at, just as we have been ridiculed. No," and here his
voice took on a new sad sureness, an air of dismal
certainty, "it is meant that if they don't prepare,
they die. I see no need for further argument." And
so she had reluctantly acquiesced.

With seven minutes left, the first knock rang the
shelter door. "Let us in! For God's sake, man, let
us in!"

He recognized the voice. It was his first neighbor
down the road toward town.

"No!" shouted the father. "There is only room
for us. Go! Take shelter in your homes. You may
yet be spared."

Again came the pounding. Louder. More urgent.
"You let us in or we'll break down this door!"
He wondered, with some concern, if they were
actually getting a ram of some sort to batter at the
door. He was reasonably certain it would hold. At
least as long as it must.

The seconds ticked relentlessly away. Four minutes left.

His wife stared at the door in stricken fascination
and moaned slightly. "Steady, girl," he said evenly.
The children, having halted their game at the first
shouting, looked at him in fearful wonderment. He
glared at his watch, ran his hands distraughtly
through his hair and said nothing.

Three minutes left.

At that moment, a woman's cry from the outside
pierced him in an utterly vulnerable spot, a place
the men could never have touched with their des-
perate demands. "If you won't let me in," she
cried, "please take my baby, my little girl."

He was stunned by her plea. This he had not
anticipated. What must I do? he asked himself in
sheer agony. What man on earth could deny a child
the chance to live?

At that point, his wife rose, sobbing, and stepped

to the door. Before he could move to stop her, she let down the latch and dashed outside. Instantly a three-year-old girl was thrust into the shelter. He hastily fought the door latch on again, then stared at the frightened little newcomer in mute rage, hating her with an abstract hatred for simply being there in his wife's place and knowing he could not turn her out.

He sat down heavily, trying desperately to think. The voices outside grew louder. He glanced at his watch, looked at the faces of his own children a long moment, then rose to his feet. There were two minutes left, and he had made his decision. He marveled now that he had even considered any other choice.

"Son," he said to the older boy, "you take care of them." It was as simple as that.

Unlatching the door, he thrust it open and stepped out. The crowd surged toward him. Blocking the door with his body, he snatched up the two children nearest him, a boy and a girl, and shoved them into the shelter. "Bar that door," he shouted to his son, "and don't open it for at least a week!"

Hearing the latch drop into place, he turned and glanced around at the faces in the crowd. Some of them were still babbling incoherently, utterly panic-stricken. Others were quiet now, resigned, no longer afraid.

Stepping to his wife's side, he took her hand and spoke in a warm, low tone. "They will be all right; the boy will lead them." He grinned reassuringly and added, "We should be together, you and I."

She smiled wordlessly through her tears and squeezed his hand, exchanging with him in the one brief gesture a lifetime and more of devotion.

Then struck the first bomb, blinding them, burning them, blasting them into eternity. Streaking across the top of the world, across the extreme

northern tip of Greenland, then flaming downrange
through the chilled arctic skies, it had passed over
Moscow, over Voronezh and on over Krasny to
detonate high above their city of Shakhty.

The bird had been 19 minutes in flight, launched
from a bomb-blasted, seared-surface missile pit on
the coast of California. America's retaliation continued for several hours.

Puppet Show

fredric brown

Horror came to Cherrybell at a little after noon on a blistering hot day in August.

Perhaps that is redundant; *any* August day in Cherrybell, Arizona, is blistering hot. It is on Highway 89, about 40 miles south of Tucson and about 30 miles north of the Mexican border. It consists of two filling stations, one on each side of the road to catch travelers going in both directions, a general store, a beer-and-wine-license-only tavern, a tourist-trap-type trading post for tourists who can't wait until they reach the border to start buying serapes and huaraches, a deserted hamburger stand, and a few 'dobe houses inhabited by Mexican-Americans who work in Nogales, the border town to the south, and who, for God knows what reason, prefer to live in Cherrybell and commute, some of them in Model T Fords. The sign on the highway says, CHERRYBELL, POP. 42, but the sign exaggerates; Pop died last year—Pop Anders, who ran the now-deserted hamburger stand—and the correct figure should be 41.

Horror came to Cherrybell mounted on a burro led by an ancient, dirty and gray-bearded desert rat of a prospector who later gave the name of Dade

161

Grant. Horror's name was Garvane. He was approximately nine feet tall but so thin, almost a stickman, that he could not have weighed over a hundred pounds. Old Dade's burro carried him easily, despite the fact that his feet dragged in the sand on either side. Being dragged through the sand for, as it later turned out, well over five miles hadn't caused the slightest wear on the shoes—more like buskins, they were—which constituted all that he wore except for a pair of what could have been swimming trunks, in robin's-egg blue. But it wasn't his dimensions that made him horrible to look upon, it was his *skin*. It looked red, raw. It looked as though he had been skinned alive and the skin replaced raw side out. His skull, his face were equally narrow or elongated; otherwise, in every visible way, he appeared human—or at least humanoid. Unless you count such little things as the fact that his hair was robin's-egg blue to match his trunks, as were his eyes and his boots. Blood red and light blue.

Casey, owner of the tavern, was the first one to see them coming across the plain from the direction of the mountain range to the east. He'd stepped out of the back door of his tavern for a breath of fresh, if hot, air. They were about a hundred yards away at that time, and already he could see the utter alienness of the figure on the led burro. Just alienness at that distance; the horror came only at closer range. Casey's jaw dropped and stayed down until the strange trio was about 50 yards away; then he started slowly toward them. There are people who run at the sight of the unknown, others who advance to meet it. Casey advanced, slowly, to meet it.

Still in the wide open, 20 yards from the back of the little tavern, he met them. Dade Grant stopped and dropped the rope by which he was leading the burro. The burro stood still and dropped its head. The stickman stood up simply by planting his feet solidly and standing astride the burro. He stepped one leg across it and stood a moment, leaning his weight against his hands on the burro's back, and then sat down in the sand. "High-gravity planet," he said. "Can't stand long."

"Kin I get water fer my burro?" the prospector asked Casey. "Must be purty thirsty by now. Hadda leave water bags, some other things so it could carry——" He jerked a thumb toward the red-and-blue horror.

Casey was just realizing that it *was* a horror. At a distance the color combination seemed only mildly hideous, but close up—the skin was rough and seemed to have veins on the outside and looked moist (although it wasn't) and *damn* if it didn't look just like he had his skin peeled off and put back on inside out. Or just peeled off, period. Casey had never seen anything like it and hoped he wouldn't ever see anything like it again.

Casey felt something behind him and looked over his shoulder. Others had seen now and were coming, but the nearest of them, a pair of boys, were ten yards behind him. "*Muchachos*," he called out. "*Agua por el burro. Un pozal. Pronto.*"

He looked back and said, "What—— Who——"

"Name's Dade Grant," said the prospector, putting out a hand, which Casey took absently. When he let go of it, it jerked back over the desert rat's shoulder, thumb indicating the thing that sat on the sand. "*His* name's Garvane, he tells me. He's an extra something or other, and he's some kind of minister."

Casey nodded at the stickman and was glad to get a nod in return instead of an extended hand. "I'm Manuel Casey," he said. "What does he mean, an extra something?"

The stickman's voice was unexpectedly deep and

vibrant. "I am an extraterrestrial. And a minister plenipotentiary."

Surprisingly, Casey was a moderately well educated man and knew both of those phrases; he was probably the only person in Cherrybell who would have known the second one. Less surprisingly, considering the speaker's appearance, he believed both of them.

"What can I do for you, sir?" he asked. "But first, why not come in out of the sun?"

"No, thank you. It's a bit cooler here than they told me it would be, but I'm quite comfortable. This is equivalent to a cool spring evening on my planet. And as to what you can do for me, you can notify your authorities of my presence. I believe they will be interested."

Well, Casey thought, by blind luck he's hit the best man for his purpose within at least 20 miles. Manuel Casey was half Irish, half Mexican. He had a half brother who was half Irish and half assorted American, and the half brother was a bird colonel at Davis-Monthan Air Force Base in Tucson.

He said, "Just a minute, Mr. Garvane, I'll telephone. You, Mr. Grant, would you want to come inside?"

"Naw, I don't mind sun. Out in it all day ever' day. An' Garvane here, he ast me if I'd stick with him till he was finished with what he's gotta do here. Said he'd gimme somethin' purty vallable if I did. Somethin'—a 'lectrononic——"

"An electronic battery-operated portable ore indicator," Garvane said. "A simple little device, indicates presence of a concentration of ore up to two miles, indicates kind, grade, quantity and depth."

Casey gulped, excused himself and pushed through the gathering crowd into his tavern. He had Colonel Casey on the phone in one minute, but it took him another four minutes to convince the colonel that he was neither drunk nor joking.

Twenty-five minutes after that, there was a noise in the sky, a noise that swelled and then died as a four-man helicopter sat down and shut off its rotors a dozen yards from an extraterrestrial, two men and a burro. Casey alone had had the courage to rejoin the trio from the desert; there were other spectators, but they still held well back.

Colonel Casey, a major, a captain and a lieutenant who was the helicopter's pilot all came out and ran over. The stickman stood up, all nine feet of him; from the effort it cost him to stand you could tell that he was used to a much lighter gravity than Earth's. He bowed, repeated his name and the identification of himself as an extraterrestrial and a minister plenipotentiary. Then he apologized for sitting down again, explained why it was necessary and sat down.

The colonel introduced himself and the three who had come with him. "And now, sir, what can we do for you?"

The stickman made a grimace that was probably intended as a smile. His teeth were the same light blue as his hair and eyes.

"You have a cliché, 'Take me to your leader.' I do not ask that. In fact, I *must* remain here. Nor do I ask that any of your leaders be brought here to me. That would be impolite. I am perfectly willing for you to represent them, to talk to you and let you question me. But I do ask one thing.

"You have tape recorders. I ask that before I talk or answer questions, you have one brought. I want to be sure that the message your leaders eventually receive is full and accurate."

"Fine," the colonel said. He turned to the pilot. "Lieutenant, get on the radio in the whirlybird and tell them to get us a tape recorder faster than possible. It can be dropped by para—— No, that'd take longer, rigging it for a drop. Have them send it by another helicopter." The lieutenant turned to go. "Hey," the colonel said, "also fifty yards of extension cord. We'll have to plug it in inside Manny's tavern."

The lieutenant sprinted for the helicopter.

The others sat and sweated a moment and then Manuel Casey stood up. "That's a half-an-hour wait," he said, "and if we're going to sit here in the sun, who's for a bottle of cold beer? You, Mr. Garvane?"

"It is a cold beverage, is it not? I am a bit chilly. If you have something hot——"

"Coffee, coming up. Can I bring you a blanket?"

"No, thank you. It will not be necessary."

Casey left and shortly returned with a tray with half a dozen bottles of cold beer and a cup of steaming coffee. The lieutenant was back by then. Casey put the tray down and served the stickman first, who sipped the coffee and said, "It is delicious."

Colonel Casey cleared his throat, "Serve our prospector friend next, Manny. As for us—well, drinking is forbidden on duty, but it was a hundred and twelve in the shade in Tucson, and this is hotter and also is *not* in the shade. Gentlemen, consider yourselves on official leave for as long as it takes you to drink one bottle of beer or until the tape recorder arrives, whichever comes first."

The beer was finished first, but by the time the last of it had vanished, the second helicopter was within sight and sound. Casey asked the stickman if he wanted more coffee. The offer was politely declined. Casey looked at Dade Grant and winked, and the desert rat winked back; so Casey went in for two more bottles, one apiece for the civilian terrestrials. Coming back, he met the lieutenant arriving with the extension cord and returned as far as the doorway to show him where to plug it in.

When he came back, he saw that the second helicopter had brought its full complement of four, besides the tape recorder. There were, besides the pilot who had flown it, a technical sergeant who was skilled in its operation and who was now making adjustments on it and a lieutenant colonel and a warrant officer who had come along for the ride or because they had been made curious by the *request* for a tape recorder to be rushed to Cherrybell, Arizona, by air. They were standing gaping at the stickman, and whispered conversations were going on.

The colonel said, "Attention," quietly, but it brought complete silence. "Please sit down, gentlemen. In a rough circle. Sergeant, if you rig your mike in the center of the circle, will it pick up clearly what any one of us may say?"

"Yes, sir. I'm almost ready."

Ten men and one extraterrestrial humanoid sat in a rough circle, with the microphone hanging from a small tripod in the approximate center. The humans were sweating profusely; the humanoid shivered slightly. Just outside the circle, the burro stood dejectedly, its head low. Edging closer, but still about five yards away, spread out now in a semicircle, was the entire population of Cherrybell who had been at home at the time; the stores and the filling stations were deserted.

The technical sergeant pushed a button and the tape recorder's reel started to turn. "Testing . . . testing," he said. He held down the rewind button for a second and then pushed the playback button. "Testing . . . testing," said the recorder's speaker. Loud and clear. The sergeant pushed the rewind button, then the erase one to clear the tape. Then the stop button.

"When I push the next button, sir," he said to the colonel, "we'll be recording."

The colonel looked at the tall extraterrestrial, who nodded, and then the colonel nodded at the sergeant. The sergeant pushed the recording button.

"My name is Garvane," said the stickman slowly and clearly. "I am from a planet of a star which is not listed in your star catalogs, although the globular cluster in which it is one of ninety thousand stars is known to you. It is, from here, in the direction of the center of the galaxy at a distance of over four thousand light-years.

"However, I am not here as a representative of my planet or my people, but as minister plenipotentiary of the Galactic Union, a federation of the enlightened civilizations of the galaxy, for the good of all. It is my assignment to visit you and decide, here and now, whether or not you are to be welcomed to join our federation.

"You may now ask questions freely. However, I reserve the right to postpone answering some of them until my decision has been made. If the decision is favorable, I will then answer all questions, including the ones I have postponed answering meanwhile. Is that satisfactory?"

"Yes," said the colonel. "How did you come here? A spaceship?"

"Correct. It is overhead right now, in orbit twenty-two thousand miles out, so it revolves with the Earth and stays over this one spot. I am under observation from it, which is one reason I prefer to remain here in the open. I am to signal it when I want it to come down to pick me up."

"How do you know our language so fluently? Are you telepathic?"

"No, I am not. And nowhere in the galaxy is any race telepathic except among its own members. I was taught your language for this purpose. We have had observers among you for many centuries— by *we*, I mean the Galactic Union, of course. Quite obviously, I could not pass as an Earthman, but there are other races who can. Incidentally, they are not spies or agents; they have in no way tried to affect you; they are observers and that is all."

"What benefits do we get from joining your union,

if we are asked and if we accept?" the colonel asked.

"First, a quick course in the fundamental social sciences which will end your tendency to fight among yourselves and end or at least control your aggressions. After we are satisfied that you have accomplished that and it is safe for you to do so, you will be given space travel and many other things as rapidly as you are able to assimilate them."

"And if we are not asked or refuse?"

"Nothing. You will be left alone; even our observers will be withdrawn. You will work out your own fate—either you will render your planet uninhabited and uninhabitable within the next century or you will master social science yourselves and again be candidates for membership and again be offered membership. We will check from time to time, and if and when it appears certain that you are not going to destroy yourselves, you will again be approached."

"Why the hurry, now that you're here? Why can't you stay long enough for our leaders, as you call them, to talk to you in person?"

"Postponed. The reason is not important but it is complicated, and I simply do not wish to waste time explaining."

"Assuming your decision is favorable, how will we get in touch with you to let you know *our* decision? You know enough about us, obviously, to know that *I* can't make it."

"We will know your decision through our observers. One condition of acceptance is full and uncensored publication in your newspapers of this interview, verbatim from the tape we are now using to record it. Also of all deliberations and decisions of your government."

"And other governments? We can't decide unilaterally for the world."

"Your government has been chosen for a start. If

you accept, we shall furnish the techniques that will cause the others to fall in line quickly—and those techniques do not involve force or the threat of force."

"They must be *some* techniques," said the colonel wryly, "if they'll make one certain country I don't have to name fall into line without even a threat."

"Sometimes the offer of reward is more significant than the use of a threat. Do you think the country you do not wish to name would like your country colonizing planets of far stars before they even reach the moon? But that is a minor point, relatively. You may trust the techniques."

"It sounds almost too good to be true. But you said that you are to decide, here and now, whether or not we are to be invited to join. May I ask on what factors you will base your decision?"

"One is that I am—was, since I already have—to check your degree of xenophobia. In the loose sense in which you use it, that means fear of strangers. We have a word that has no counterpart in your vocabulary; it means fear of and revulsion toward *aliens*. I—or at least a member of my race—was chosen to make the first overt contact with you. Because I am what you would call roughly humanoid—as you are what I would call roughly humanoid—I am probably more horrible, more repulsive, to you than many completely different species would be. Because to you I am a caricature of a human being, I am more horrible to you than a being who bears no remote resemblance to you.

"You may think you *do* feel horror at me, and revulsion, but believe me, you have passed that test. There *are* races in the galaxy who can never be members of the federation, no matter how they advance otherwise, because they are violently and incurably xenophobic; they could never face or talk to an alien of any species. They would either run screaming from him or try to kill him instantly.

From watching you and these people"—he waved a long arm at the civilian population of Cherrybell not far outside the circle of the conference—"I know you feel revulsion at the sight of me, but believe me, it is relatively slight and certainly curable. You have passed that test satisfactorily."

"And are there other tests?"

"One other. But I think it is time that I——" Instead of finishing the sentence, the stickman lay back flat on the sand and closed his eyes.

The colonel started to his feet. "What in *hell*?" he said. He walked quickly around the mike's tripod and bent over the recumbent extraterrestrial, putting an ear to the bloody-appearing chest.

As he raised his head, Dade Grant, the grizzled prospector, chuckled. "No heartbeat, Colonel, because no heart. But I may leave him as a souvenir for you and you'll find much more interesting things inside him than heart and guts. Yes, he is a puppet whom I have been operating, as your Edgar Bergen operates his—what's his name?—oh, yes, Charlie McCarthy. Now that he has served his purpose, he is deactivated. You can go back to your place, Colonel."

Colonel Casey moved back slowly. *"Why?"* he asked.

Dade Grant was peeling off his beard and wig. He rubbed a cloth across his face to remove make-up and was revealed as a handsome young man. He said, "What he told you, or what you were told through him, was true as far as it went. He is only a simulacrum, yes, but he is an exact duplicate of a member of one of the intelligent races of the galaxy, the one toward whom you would be disposed—if you were violently and incurably xenophobic—to be most horrified by, according to our psychologists. But we did not bring a real member of his species to make first contact because they have a phobia of their own, agoraphobia—fear of space.

They are highly civilized and members in good standing of the federation, but they never leave their own planet.

"Our observers assure us you don't have *that* phobia. But they were unable to judge in advance the degree of your xenophobia, and the only way to test it was to bring along something in lieu of someone to test it against and presumably to let him make the initial contact."

The colonel sighed audibly. "I can't say this doesn't relieve me in one way. We could get along with humanoids, yes, and we will when we have to. But I'll admit it's a relief to learn that the master race of the galaxy is, after all, human instead of only humanoid. What is the second test?"

"You are undergoing it now. Call me——" He snapped his fingers. "What's the name of Bergen's second-string puppet, after Charlie McCarthy?"

The colonel hesitated, but the tech sergeant supplied the answer. "Mortimer Snerd."

"Right. So call me Mortimer Snerd, and now I think it is time that I——" He lay back flat on the sand and closed his eyes just as the stickman had done a few minutes before.

The burro raised its head and put it into the circle over the shoulder of the tech sergeant.

"That takes care of the puppets, Colonel," it said. "And now, what's this bit about it being important that the master race be human or at least humanoid? What is a master race?"

Papa's Planet

william f. nolan

Of the late Harrington Hunter Hollister it must be said that he was very rich, that he had sired a beautiful man-chasing redhead and that he was a Hemingway fanatic. When he died, in 2068, I ended up with his money, his newly divorced daughter and his Hemingway collection.

"As my latest and absolutely *last* husband, I want you to have everything," Cecile Hollister told me, wrinkling her attractively freckled nose. "Daddy adored you."

"I adored daddy," I said, trying for sincerity.

She handed me a rolled parchment.

"What's this?" I asked.

"A deed to Papa's Planet. I've never been there, but daddy told me all about it. That's where we're spending our honeymoon."

"We are?"

"You want to see your property, don't you?"

"I guess so."

"We'll leave tomorrow."

Cecile had a way with men.

We left tomorrow.

• • •

Five million miles out from Mars, we turned sharp left and there it was: Papa's Planet—a big gray ball of matter floating below us.

"What the devil's *down* there?" I asked.

"You'll find out. Strap in. Here we go."

We made a fine soft-point landing (Cecile could handle a Spacer like a pro) and, when the rocket smoke cleared, I saw a big, wide-chested fellow in khaki hunting clothes approaching us. He was bearded, grizzled, with suspicious eyes. And he carried an elephant gun.

"You critics?" he demanded.

"Nope," said Cecile. "I'm the daughter of Harrington Hollister and this is my new husband, Philip."

"OK, then," said the bearded man, pivoting. "I'm hunting critics. See any, give me a yell."

"Will do," said Cecile. And to me: "C'mon, Pamplona should be right on the other side of the mountain. We can catch the running of the bulls."

"Who was the aggressive bearded guy?"

"Papa, of course. It's his planet."

* * *

Running along next to me, just in front of the bulls, a strong-looking guy thumped my shoulder and yelled, "This is swell, isn't it!"

"Yeah, swell!" I yelled back, sprinting to catch Cecile. "Who's the guy back there, yelling?"

"Papa," she told me. "Only he's a lot younger, naturally. This is 1923. Hey, let's cut through this side street. I want to see Paris."

Paris was right next to Pamplona, and Cecile looked radiant walking down the Rue de la Paix. "I'd like to meet Gertrude Stein," she said. "Maybe we can have lunch with her."

A big guy with a mustache pounded past us in a half crouch, feinting at the air with left and right jabs. He was dark-haired, tough-looking. "Hi, daughter," he said to Cecile.

"Hi, Ernie," she called back.

He padded away.

"Wait a damn minute," I said. "Who was *that*?"

She sighed. "Papa, naturally. Only nobody calls him Papa in Paris. Too early. Wrong period."

"Just how many Papas *are* there?"

Cecile stopped and wrinkled her nose. "Well, let's see . . . at least twenty that I know of, and I'm no expert. That was daddy's department."

"And they're *all* here?"

"Sure." She pointed. "Just beyond Paris, across the Seine, is Oak Park, Illinois—which is next to Walloon Lake, Michigan. That's two Papas right there, one for each place. Both are *boy* Papas, of course. One goes to Oak Park High and the other goes trout fishing on the lake."

I nodded. "We've got one here—and another in Pamplona. And there's the one we met near the rocket."

"That was the African one," she said. "Then there's the one in New York with the hairy chest who keeps standing Max Eastman on his head in the corner at Scribner's. And the Papa in the hills of Spain covering the civil war and the one skiing in Switzerland with Hadley and the one on the Gulf Stream in the *Pilar*—daddy dug out a lovely Gulf Stream and I can't wait to see it—and there's the one getting shot in the kneecap somewhere in Italy."

"Fossalta di Piave," I supplied.

"That's the place," she said, pushing back a strand of delicious red hair. "And there's the Papa in Key West and the one in Venice and the one boxing in the gym in Kansas City. How many is that?"

"I've lost count," I said.

"Anyway, there are *lots* more," said Cecile. "Daddy had his whole factory in Des Moines working overtime for six months, including weekends, just to supply all the Papas."

"Probably one camped out by the big Two-Hearted River."

"Sure. And another in Toronto, working for the *Star*."

I raised an eyebrow. "Must have cost your dad plenty."

"It was a tax write-off," she said. "Nonprofit. Besides, he had this big empty planet just going to *waste* up here."

"But—building Paris in the Twenties and the streets of Pamplona and the bull rings of Spain—and all of Africa——"

"He didn't build *all* of Africa," Cecile corrected me. "Just the important part around Kilimanjaro, where we landed."

"Don't the Papas get mixed up, bump into each other?"

"Never. Each Papa has his assigned place and that's where he stays, doing what he was built for. The Pamplona Papa just keeps running with the bulls, and the African Papa keeps hunting critics."

"Your father sure didn't stint."

"When daddy did a thing, he did it *right*," she agreed. "Now let's go have lunch with Miss Stein and then visit Venice. Daddy said they did a marvelous job with St. Mark's Square."

• • •

Papa was drinking alone at a table near the Grand Canal when our gondola passed by, and he waved us over.

"You smell good, daughter," Papa told Cecile. "You smell the way good leather you find in the little no-nonsense shops in Madrid when you know enough not to get suckered into the big shops that charge too much smells."

"Thanks, Papa," said Cecile, giving him a bright smile.

"I always enjoy the Gritti here in Venice," said Papa, "and ordering a strong lobster who had much heart and who died properly and having him served to you by a waiter you can trust with the fine good bottle of Capri near you so you can see the little green ice bubbles form on the cold glass."

He poured us wine. We all saluted one another and drank. The sun went down and the wine made me sleepy.

When I awoke, Cecile was gone.

I said good-bye to Papa and went out to look for her.

• • •

She wasn't at Key West, or on the Gulf, or anywhere in Spain, or in Billings, Montana (where Papa was recovering from his auto accident). I finally found her in Paris. On the Left Bank.

"I've fallen in love," she declared. "You can go on back to Earth and forget me."

I shrugged. Cecile was hardly steadfast; as her fourth husband, I realized that. "Who is he?"

"I call him Ougly-poo. That's my special love name for him. He just adores it."

"He isn't human, is he?"

"Of course not!" She looked annoyed. "We're the only *people* on Papa's Planet. But what difference does that make?"

"No difference, I guess."

"He's divine." She smiled dreamily, wrinkling her freckles. "Kind of a classic profile, soft, sensitive lips, exciting eyes. . . . He gave me this autographed picture. See?"

I looked at it. "You're sure?"

"I'm sure," she said.

"OK, then," I said. " 'Bye, Cecile."

" 'Bye, Philip." She threw me a kiss.

I walked back to the rocket through a sad, softly falling Hemingway rain. I didn't blame Cecile. The fellow was handsome, witty, brilliant, famous. All the things I wasn't. Girls weren't inspired to call me Ougly-poo.

But then, I wasn't F. Scott Fitzgerald.

Dial "F" for Frankenstein

arthur c. clarke

At 0150 Greenwich Mean Time on December 1, 1975, every telephone in the world started to ring. A quarter of a billion people picked up their receivers to listen for a few seconds with annoyance or perplexity. Those who had been awakened in the middle of the night assumed that some far-off friend was calling over the satellite telephone network that had gone into service, with such a blaze of publicity, the day before. But there was no voice on the line, only a sound that to many seemed like the roaring of the sea—to others, like the vibrations of harp strings in the wind. And there were many more, in that moment, who recalled a secret sound of childhood—the noise of blood pulsing through the veins, heard when a shell is cupped over the ear. Whatever it was, it lasted no more than 20 seconds; then it was replaced by the dialing tone.

The world's subscribers cursed, muttered, "Wrong number," and hung up. Some tried to dial a complaint, but the line seemed busy. In a few hours, everyone had forgotten the incident—except those whose duty it was to worry about such things.

At the Post Office Research Station, the argument had been going on all morning and had got nowhere. It continued unabated through the lunch break, when the hungry engineers poured into the little café across the road.

"I still think," said Willy Smith, the solid-state electronics man, "that it was a temporary surge of current, caused when the satellite network was switched in."

"It was obviously *something* to do with the satellites," agreed Jules Reyner, circuit designer. "But why the time delay? They were plugged in at midnight; the ringing was two hours later—as we all know to our cost." He yawned violently.

"What do *you* think, Doc?" asked Bob Andrews, computer programmer. "You've been very quiet all morning. Surely you've got some idea?"

Dr. John Williams, head of the mathematics division, stirred uneasily.

"Yes," he said, "I have. But you won't take it seriously."

"That doesn't matter. Even if it's as crazy as those science-fiction yarns you write under a pseudonym, it may give us some leads."

Williams blushed, but not very hard. Everyone knew about his stories, and he wasn't ashamed of them. After all, they *had* been collected in book form. (Remainder at five shillings; he still had a couple of hundred copies.)

"Very well," he said, doodling on the tablecloth. "This is something I've been wondering about for years. Have you ever considered the analogy between an automatic telephone exchange and the human brain?"

"Who hasn't thought of it?" scoffed one of his listeners. "That idea must go back to Graham Bell."

"Possibly; I never said it was original. But I do say it's time we started taking it seriously." He squinted balefully at the fluorescent tubes above the table; they were needed on this foggy winter day. "What's wrong with the damn lights? They've been flickering for the last five minutes."

"Don't bother about that; Maisie's probably forgotten to pay her electricity bill. Let's hear more about your theory."

"Most of it isn't theory; it's plain fact. We know that the human brain is a system of switches—neurons—interconnected in a very elaborate fashion by nerves. An automatic telephone exchange is also a system of switches—selectors, and so forth—connected together with wires."

"Agreed," said Smith. "But that analogy won't get you very far. Aren't there about fifteen billion neurons in the brain? That's a lot more than the number of switches in an autoexchange."

Williams's answer was interrupted by the scream of a low-flying jet; he had to wait until the café had ceased to vibrate before he could continue.

"Never heard them fly *that* low," Andrews grumbled. "Thought it was against regulations."

"So it is, but don't worry—London Airport Control will catch him."

"I doubt it," said Reyner. "That *was* London Airport, bringing in a Concorde on ground approach. But I've never heard one so low, either. Glad I wasn't aboard."

"Are we, or are we *not,* going to get on with this blasted discussion?" demanded Smith.

"You're right about the fifteen billion neurons in the human brain," continued Williams, unabashed. "And *that's* the whole point. Fifteen billion sounds a large number, but it isn't. Round about the 1960s, there were more than that number of individual switches in the world's autoexchanges. Today, there are approximately five times as many."

"I see," said Reyner very slowly. "And as of yesterday, they've all become capable of full interconnection, now that the satellite links have gone into service."

"Precisely."

There was silence for a moment, apart from the distant clanging of a fire-engine bell.

"Let me get this straight," said Smith. "Are you suggesting that the world telephone system is now a giant brain?"

"That's putting it crudely—anthropomorphically. I prefer to think of it in terms of critical size." Williams held his hands out in front of him, fingers partly closed.

"Here are two lumps of U 235; nothing happens as long as you keep them apart. But bring them together"—he suited the action to the words—"and you have something *very* different from one bigger lump of uranium. You have a hole half a mile across.

"It's the same with our telephone networks; until today they've been largely independent, autonomous. But now we've suddenly multiplied the connecting links—the networks have all merged together—and we've reached criticality."

"And just what does criticality mean in this case?" asked Smith.

"For want of a better word—consciousness."

"A weird sort of consciousness," said Reyner. "What would it use for sense organs?"

"Well, all the radio and TV stations in the world would be feeding information into it, through their landlines. *That* should give it something to think about! Then there would be all the data stored in all the computers; it would have access to that—and to the electronic libraries, the radar tracking systems, the telemetering in the automatic factories. Oh, it would have enough sense organs! We can't begin to imagine its picture of the world, but it would certainly be infinitely richer and more complex than ours."

"Granted all this, because it's an entertaining idea," said Reyner, "what could it *do* except think? It couldn't go anywhere; it would have no limbs."

"Why should it want to travel? It would already be everywhere! And every piece of remotely controlled electrical equipment on the planet could act as a limb."

"Now I understand that time delay," interjected Andrews. "It was conceived at midnight, but it wasn't born until one-fifty this morning. The noise that woke us all up was—its birth cry."

His attempt to sound facetious was not altogether convincing, and nobody smiled. Overhead, the lights continued their annoying flicker, which seemed to be getting worse. Then there was an interruption from the front of the café as Jim Small of Power Supplies made his usual boisterous entry.

"Look at this, fellows," he grinned, waving a piece of paper in front of his colleagues. "I'm rich. Ever seen a bank balance like *that*?"

Dr. Williams took the proffered statement, glanced down the columns and read the balance aloud: "Credit £999,999,897.87.

"Nothing very odd about that," he continued above the general amusement. "I'd say it means the computer's made a slight mistake. That sort of thing was happening all the time just after the banks converted to the decimal system."

"I know, I know," said Jim, "but don't spoil my fun. I'm going to frame this statement—and what would happen if I drew a check for a few million on the strength of this? Could I sue the bank if it bounced?"

"Not on your life," answered Reyner. "I'll take a bet that the banks thought of *that* years ago and protected themselves somewhere down in the small print.

But by the way—when did you get that statement?"

"In the noon delivery; it comes straight to the office, so that my wife doesn't have a chance of seeing it."

"Hmm—that means it was computed early this morning. Certainly after midnight. . . ."

"What are you driving at? And why all the long faces?"

No one answered him; he had started a new hare, and the hounds were in full cry.

"Does anyone here know about automated banking systems?" asked Willy Smith. "How are they tied together?"

"Like everything else these days," said Bob Andrews. "They're all in the same network—the computers talk to one another all over the world. It's a point for you, John. If there *was* real trouble, that's one of the first places I'd expect it. Besides the phone system itself, of course."

"No one answered the question I asked before Jim came in," complained Reyner. "What would this supermind actually *do*? Would it be friendly—hostile —indifferent? Would it even know that we exist, or would it consider the electronic signals it's handling to be the only reality?"

"I see you're beginning to believe me," said Williams with a certain grim satisfaction. "I can only answer your question by asking another. What does a newborn baby do? It starts looking for food." He glanced up at the flickering lights. "My God," he said slowly, as if a thought had just struck him. "There's only one food it would need—electricity."

"This nonsense has gone far enough," said Smith. "What the devil's happened to our lunch? We gave our orders twenty minutes ago."

Everyone ignored him.

"And then," said Reyner, taking up where Williams had left off, "it would start looking around and stretching its limbs. In fact, it would start to play, like any growing baby."

"And babies *break* things," said someone softly.

"It would have enough toys, heaven knows. That Concorde that went over just now. The automated production lines. The traffic lights in our streets."

"Funny you should mention that," interjected Small. "Something's happened to the traffic outside —it's been stopped for the last ten minutes. Looks like a big jam."

"I guess there's a fire somewhere—I heard an engine."

"I've heard two—and what sounded like an explosion over toward the industrial estate. Hope it's nothing serious."

"Maisie!!! What about some candles? We can't see a thing!"

"I've just remembered—this place has an all-electric kitchen. We're going to get cold lunch, if we get any lunch at all."

"At least we can read the newspaper while we're waiting. Is that the latest edition you've got there, Jim?"

"Yes—haven't had time to look at it yet. Hmm— there *do* seem to have been a lot of odd accidents this morning—railway signals jammed—water main blown up through failure of relief valve—dozens of complaints about last night's wrong numbers——"

He turned the page and became suddenly silent.

"What's the matter?"

Without a word, Small handed over the paper. Only the front page made sense. Throughout the interior, column after column was a mass of printer's pie—with, here and there, a few incongruous advertisements making islands of sanity in a sea of gibberish. They had obviously been set up as independent blocks and had escaped the scrambling that had overtaken the text around them.

"So this is where long-distance typesetting and autodistribution have brought us," grumbled Andrews. "I'm afraid Fleet Street's been putting too many eggs in one electronic basket."

"So have we all, I'm afraid," said Williams very solemnly. "So have we all."

"If I can get a word in edgeways, in time to stop the mob hysteria which seems to be infecting this table," said Smith loudly and firmly, "I'd like to point out that there's nothing to worry about—even if John's ingenious fantasy is correct. We only have to switch off the satellites—and we'll be back where we were yesterday."

"Prefrontal lobotomy," muttered Williams. "I'd thought of that."

"Eh? Oh, yes—cutting out slabs of the brain. That would certainly do the trick. Expensive, of course, and we'd have to go back to sending telegrams to each other. But civilization would survive."

From not too far away, there was a short, sharp explosion.

"I don't like this," said Andrews nervously. "Let's hear what the old BBC's got to say—the one-o'clock news has just started."

He reached into his briefcase and pulled out a transistor radio.

"—unprecedented number of industrial accidents, as well as the unexplained launching of three salvos of guided missiles from military installations in the United States. Several airports have had to suspend operations owing to the erratic behavior of their radars, and the banks and stock exchanges have closed because their information-processing systems have become completely unreliable." ("You're telling me," muttered Small, while the others shushed him.) "One moment, please—there's a news flash coming

through. . . . Here it is. We have just been informed
that all control over the newly installed communica-
tion satellites has been lost. They are no longer
responding to commands from the ground. According to——"

The BBC went off the air; even the carrier wave
died. Andrews reached for the tuning knob and
twisted it round the dial. Over the whole band, the
ether was silent.

Presently Reyner said, in a voice not far from
hysteria, "That prefrontal lobotomy was a good idea,
John. Too bad that baby's already thought of it."

Williams rose slowly to his feet.

"Let's get back to the lab," he said. "There must
be an answer somewhere."

But he knew already that it was far, far too late.
For Homo sapiens, the telephone bell had tolled.

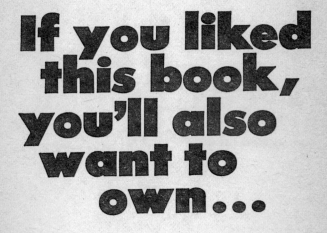

If you liked
this book,
you'll also
want to
own...

TRANSIT OF EARTH

Thirteen science-fiction stories by such masters of the genre as

**Arthur C. Clarke,
Ray Bradbury,
Frederik Pohl,
J. G. Ballard,
Richard Matheson,
and Fredric Brown.**

BK133   75¢

FROM THE "S" FILE

Sixteen science-fiction
stories from PLAYBOY by

**Robert Sheckley,
William Sambrot,
John Sladek,
Jack Sharkey,
Norman Spinrad,
Henry Slesar,
and Theodore Sturgeon.**

BK141   75¢

Ask your bookdealer, or order directly from:

Playboy Press
The Playboy Building
919 North Michigan Avenue
Chicago, Illinois 60611

Title	Book Number	Amount
_____	_____	_____
_____	_____	_____

(Please enclose 50¢ for postage and handling.)

_____

Total $_____

To: **Name** _____

Address _____

City _____ **State** _____ **Zip** _____